LAST CASTLE IN THE SAND

CLAREMARY P. SWEENEY

Publisher's Information

EBookBakery Books

Author contact: claremarypsweeney@yahoo.com
Author website: page https://claremarypsweeney.carrd.co
Author blog: AroundZuZusBarn.com
Cover and map design by Zachary Perry

ISBN 978-1-953080-11-0

1. Mystery 2. Claremary P. Sweeney 3. Rhode Island coastline 4. Narragansett, Rhode Island 5. Women Sleuths 6. Hazard Family 7. Matunuck 8. Shady Lea Historic District

DEDICATION

There are a hundred places where I fear
To go - so with his memory they brim.
And entering with relief some quiet place
Where never fell his foot or shone his face
I say, "There is no memory of him here!"
And so stand stricken, so remembering him.

-Edna St. Vincent Millay,
"Time Does Not Bring Relief" (Sonnet II)

Charle, To hold your hand, touch your face, and see your smile once more.

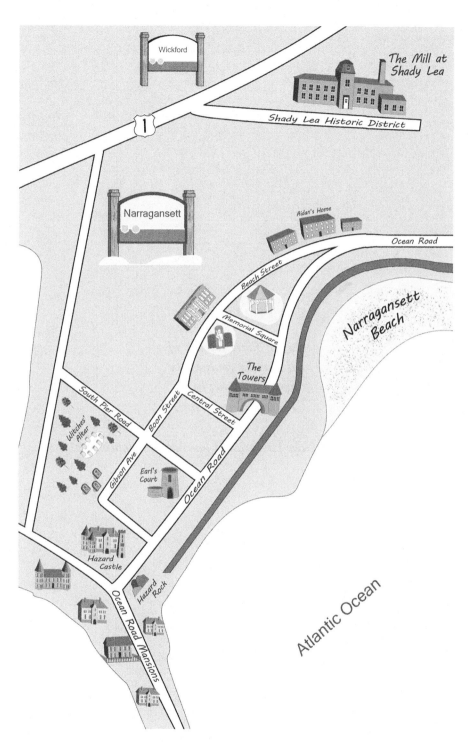

The Calm

*August Rain: the best of
the summer gone, & the
new fall not yet born.
The odd uneven time.*

-Sylvia Plath, *The Unabridged Journals of Sylvia Plath*

The heart of another is a dark forest, always,
no matter how close it has been to one's own.

-Willa Cather, *The Professor's House*

IN LIFE'S RACE TO the finish line, death inevitably catches up to even the most entitled among us, and on this misty August evening, Dr. Morgan Duckworth's minutes were swiftly ticking away. Spying the theatre ticket on the bureau, she considered trying to make it in time for the second act, but the melodic chimes from the antique French gilt clock on her night table announced she wouldn't even catch the final curtain call.

Dropping the ticket into the wastebasket, she walked in the closet to the section where she kept her *Lululemons* and selected a dark gray jogging suit with red and black accents. She slipped off her *Mephisto Lissandra* sandals and chose her favorite pair of *Maison Margiela* running shoes to match her outfit.

Marie and Pierre Curie, her black labra doodles, sat like two statues staring at her as she applied a slight coating of foundation to her deeply tanned face. She admired her perfect features in the dressing table's mirror and added a dab of blush to highlight her well-chiseled cheekbones. *Thank you, plastic surgery.*

She chose a creamy lipstick close to the same shade as the scarlet stripe running along the outside of her pant leg. Even though she had no expectations of being seen, she always left the house prepared for any possible encounter. For a brief moment Morgan remembered her old nanny's caution about donning clean underwear to be ready in case of any unforeseen circumstances. Every time Nanny Green said the words "unforeseen circumstances" she would quickly bless herself three times. It must have worked because Morgan had never experienced any circumstances she hadn't foreseen. Slipping the *Gucci* ID lanyard over her head like a necklace, she looked at herself in the mirror, made the sign of the cross, and laughed.

She switched on the floodlights and blew air kisses to the Curies before closing the front door. She didn't bother to lock it. The house stood at the end of a long, gravel drive bordered with rhododendrons and mountain laurel; surrounded by a stone wall, gated on one side and protected by steep ocean cliffs on the other. She was confident it was well hidden from thieves. A *Tiffany* lamp in the picture window cast a soft glow. She could see the dogs now standing guard, one face in either side-lite panel of the main entrance. A light in the corner window of the third-floor nursery flickered.

Morgan began her warm-up, bending and stretching, twisting and bouncing. She'd been a world-class, distance runner in college. Her freshman year, she was offered an athletic scholarship, which her parents wouldn't allow her to accept, preferring that it be given to a "less fortunate" applicant. After her sophomore year, her mother insisted she concentrate on her studies to prepare for the profession they'd chosen for their only child – medicine. Thirty years later, she no longer practiced medicine, but she continued to run to keep in shape. It was something she was good at.

She stroked her left calf, knowing her legs still drew admiring glances from men even as her fiftieth birthday approached. She was nothing like some of the patients who'd come into her office with their constant aches and pains and persistent complaints. She'd taken pleasure in poking at their rolls of flab, telling them if they lost a few pounds, they'd feel better. To herself she added, *they'd be less disgusting for me to look at.* Dr. Morgan Duckworth didn't attempt to hide her disdain for those she deemed overweight. She abhorred fat and considered herself to be a lean, mean machine – a perfect role model for those who had sought her medical expertise.

She'd been diagnosed with an eating disorder as a teenager. Her anxious mother took her to a renowned child psychiatrist and tried to follow his advice to help Morgan overcome her anorexia. He explained how her daughter was using food to deal with uncomfortable or painful emotions.

"The girl needs to feel more in control."

Her parents were told, "Always find opportunities to reinforce anything which would promote strong self-esteem and make it a point to provide constant encouragement and praise." Finally, he cautioned them to be extra sensitive to the girl's feelings.

The Duckworths conferred over evening cocktails and concluded, after only two Cosmopolitans and a box of imported Belgian chocolates, they'd been doing this all along - from the time Morgan was born. By the third drink, however, they clicked their glasses together in a toast agreeing to try harder in order to help their daughter develop a healthier body image. Morgan was delighted in the knowledge she now had even more control over her parents than before. This could come in handy, especially with her mother.

Suddenly, she stood upright, startled upon hearing something under the port-cochere where she'd parked her silver *Alfa Romeo Spider* earlier in the day. Morgan cocked her head to listen and then dismissed it as the skittering of a mouse or a bat. The sound of a wave crashing against the rocks filled the darkness.

Outside the high stone walls and the ornate wrought-iron gate, she began her late night run east on Ocean Road toward The Towers where the wind blew a cooling, salty spray over the sea wall. She crossed the road to Memorial Square, flying past the sundial and monuments, turning on Boon Street and continuing on to Gibson. At that point, she slowed her pace and instead of going left on Earles Court toward home, she ran the short distance toward Druid's Circle. Sometimes she varied her run by veering off the road into the stand of trees to visit the witches' altar. A gentle rain had begun to fall, mingling with her sweat. Muffled thunder rolled in the distance.

The revving of a car's engine caught her attention as lights from the dead-end street up ahead came closer, accelerating past her on the opposite side of the road. It was a silver Spider exactly like hers. Behind her, the car made a U-turn. Its engine idled only for a moment. A sudden jolt of reality started her heart pounding faster. Instinct told her to rush past the graveyard toward the safety of the circle of stone columns in the woods.

She tasted salt from the moisture on her upper lip. Morgan turned. The car was heading toward her. It slowed, giving her time to leap from the shoulder of the road onto the grass. The headlights switched off before the force of the impact knocked her forward like a wave breaking against her back. She could barely breathe, as she lay pinned to the ground.

The driver stepped out and bent down close to Morgan's face. She opened her eyes. Her lids fluttered and she reached her arm up for help, like an exhausted swimmer sinking under the weight of the waves. Engulfed. Drowning. Dissolving.

A voice emanated from out of the damp stillness. "You deserve to die."

Stepping gingerly around the glass from the shattered headlight, the driver got back into the idling car - putting it into gear, turning on the parking lights, pushing down on the gas pedal before inching the Spider forward to press Morgan's prostrate form into the softened earth on the side of the road.

The iron gates to the estate were wide open. Marie and Pierre barked ecstatically to welcome the Spider home. It rolled gently into the garage. The doors closed, enveloping it in darkness. A drop of blood from its undercarriage fell onto the dirt and gravel floor.

ଔ

2

On the outskirts of every agony
sits some observant fellow who points.

- Virginia Woolf, *The Waves*

A LATE SUNDAY AFTERNOON THUNDERSHOWER had chased the few remaining tourists into the safety of their end-of-season rentals. A rainbow joined the sun toward early evening coaxing back some of the locals. Selina wiped wet sand from her hands onto the oversized towel. Its butterfly pattern still looked brand new. She'd spent precious little time lying on the beach in July and August. Not because of the weather. It had been a lovely summer in South Kingstown. One of the nicest she could remember. But then, her memory was not what it used to be - a side effect of the latest medication. So, it was possible there had been much lovelier summers from her childhood. Her head throbbed.

Selina stepped carefully around the castle she'd been building as far from the water's edge and as close to the dunes as possible without disturbing the vegetation and wildlife. Circling the sand sculpture, she'd shoveled a trench - a moat in which she'd placed a regiment of blue and green bottles – glass soldiers to protect the fragile structure it had taken hours to complete. She didn't want the ocean to come in during the night and wash it away. She closed her eyes tightly, wishing it to be there throughout the fall - long after she was gone. She removed the sunglasses to rub at her lids. *I need to cool off.*

Waves lapped at her toes, her ankles, her thighs and finally splashed gently against her chest. She glanced down. The end of her scar, like a meteor's tale, could be seen just above the bra of her swimsuit. She began to push harder against the sea, plodding through the sandy surface underfoot before ducking her head into the salt water. She stayed beneath the white caps as long as she could hold her breath, cutting through to the softly rolling waves where the early evening light glistened, blinding her - far from the distant shore.

"I think she may be in trouble." Sophia stood squinting, shading her eyes and pointing out to sea.

"Who's in trouble?" Ruth rose from the blanket to follow her friend's gaze.

"The woman who built that gigantic sandcastle." Sophia nodded to the imposing structure. The one in the *Dolce and Gabbana* bathing suit – the floral print."

Sophia Carnavale had been a model in New York City before coming to work as a pediatric nurse at South County Hospital. Gino often said she had built-in radar for expensive things. "My wife's got champagne taste," he loved to announce, pulling out the linings of his pockets to show he had no money left in them.

"Maybe I should swim out and see if she's okay?" Rick removed his tee shirt and walked toward the shoreline. It was close to Labor Day and the beach crowds had thinned. Tourists had returned to regular, everyday lives after enjoying their too brief summer vacations. The lifeguard station was deserted.

"Be careful, Honey. The undertow can be dangerous," Ruth warned.

Selina bobbed gently on the ocean's rolling surface, daydreaming. She was being carried far out to sea. Floating on her back, she imagined the white shark, recently sighted in Narragansett, had moved on to Matunuck and was watching somewhere nearby, waiting to drag her under. She felt something touching her arm. A strand of seaweed? She opened her eyes. A familiar face. She began to tread water.

"Are you okay?" he asked.

"Yes, of course." She stared into his eyes. Her memory was jarred.

"You've drifted out pretty far from shore."

"I'm an excellent swimmer. Don't you remember? Scarborough Beach?" she laughed.

"Have we met before? I'm Rick Carnavale."

"Yes, I know. I'm Selina Borelli." She waited to see if the name registered. She'd been friends with his wife Yvonne, years ago.

He concentrated a moment on her face – her perfect features. It suddenly clicked. "Selina, of course. How are you?"

"I'm fine." She brushed a strand of golden hair back from her cheek. "I was sorry to hear about Evie. She was a wonderful person."

He resisted the urge to disappear under water. "Yes, she was."

She hesitated before adding, "But then, we both know cancer doesn't give anyone a pass. Not even the best among us. I was in the hospital when I heard. I would have liked to attend her service."

For a moment, he was left speechless by thoughts of the most painful days in his past. "Yes, well, it was good to see you. If you're okay, I'm going to get back to my friends. I think they're a bit concerned." He looked to the beach where Ruth and his brother Gino were pointing at them, signaling for him to swim to shore.

"It must be nice to have people waiting for you to return."

Rick wasn't sure how to respond. "Yes, it is. Are you sure you'll be … ?"

"I'm fine. I won't stay out here much longer. Thanks." She swam away from him, as gracefully as a manta ray.

Ruth placed a towel over her husband's shoulders and looked toward the woman now swimming parallel to the beach. "Is she all right?"

"She said she was," Rick answered.

"She's probably waiting for her yacht to come along and give her a ride home," Sophia announced. Ruth gave her sister-in-law a questioning look.

"Whatsat suppose ta mean?" her husband asked.

She pointed to the spot where the woman in the water had left her things. "That is a designer towel. *Versace.* Guess how much it costs?"

"How much can a towel set cha back?" Gino waved his hands in the air.

"It's signed. Like a piece of artwork. It even has a name - *Le Jardin.* By *Ver-sa-cheee.*" Sophia emphasized the designer.

"Okay, I'm guessin bout ten bucks," her husband said.

"I'm thinking fifty?" Ruth joined in.

"Fifty bucks for a towel you trow down on da sand! Dat's crazy," Gino sputtered.

Sophia ignored this last remark and looked to Rick. "You're the artist. You want to venture a number?"

"If it's *Versace*, it must run at least a hundred." Rick had once owned an art gallery in Greenwich Village with some exclusive clients. He knew the cost of high-end products.

"You're all wrong. It'll cost you five hundred and forty smackaroos at Nordstrom's." She pulled her cell phone from her pocket. "I googled it." And those sunglasses – I recognized them. They're *Boucheron Cat Eye*." Although her modeling days were long past, Sophia still kept up with the latest styles. "Anyone want to guess what those babies will set you back?"

"I got my shades at Job Lot on sale - for four bucks," Gino told them.

"Well, for about five hundred dollars more, you can purchase a pair of *Boucherons*. But definitely not at Job Lot," Sophia said.

Gino staggered, dramatically grabbing at his chest.

"And I won't even tell you how much a *Camilla* cover-up costs at Saks." They walked to their blanket and sat down to gaze at the lone figure out in the ocean.

Gino opened the cooler looking under the last of the floating ice cubes to see if something was hiding in the bottom. "I'm stahved! Can we stop at Cap'n Jacks on the way home?"

"The point was to have a picnic on the beach and watch the sunset."

"Dat's exactly what I hate about Daylight Savings Time – for da past six months, everything's an hour later den it's sposed to be. It's not natural. It messes up my body clock," he declared.

"I don't really want to leave until I'm sure she's safe." Sophia kept her eyes on the woman in the water.

Gino popped a dripping ice cube in his mouth. "I could be dead by then. Whadya spose she does to make da kind a dough ta buy stuff like dat?"

"She's a sculptor," Rick answered his brother.

"You know her?" Ruth asked.

"Yup. Selina Borelli. She and Yvonne were in college at RISD. Selina had talent. She dropped out to get married. You might have heard of her husband - Elliot Scott. He was a pretty well-known stage actor back in the 90s."

"So, you haven't seen her for over twenty-five years and here she is, in the middle of the Atlantic Ocean, swimming off Moonstone Beach, and you recognized her?'

"Actually, she recognized me first. But, she's hard to forget. Quite stunning."

"I think she's finally coming in," Sophia announced.

Selina dried herself and put on her sunglasses and robe, picked up her tote, waved to them, and began walking along the beach toward Matunuck.

"Good news, Bro - looks like you'll live to see another day." Rick helped his brother up from the blanket.

They stopped to admire the castle in the sand and Ruth commented, "Such a marvelous piece of art. It reminds me of the Hazard Castle. It's sad to think it could be gone out with the tide by tomorrow."

%

3

The golden moments in the stream of life rush past us,
and we see nothing but sand;
the angels come to visit us,
and we only know them when they are gone.

-George Elliot, *Scenes of Clerical Life*

S ELINA QUICKENED HER PACE as she drew closer to her cottage. She wondered how long the structure would last, situated so close to the water's edge. There was less and less beachfront as mother nature and erosion sent their message of impending doom to the rich out-of-towners who'd spent millions on vacation homes to escape from their asphalt jungles in the heat of July and August. This didn't bother Selina. She knew she'd be long gone by the time the ocean tides had arrived to wash her little clapboard house out to sea.

She showered in the outside stall and left her damp bathing suit on the small enclosed porch at the back entrance. The clock on the wall let her know she would be late for tonight's performance at Theatre-By-the -Sea, even though it was close by. It didn't matter when she arrived because she'd seen *Chicago* many times. She could practically recite the first act of the musical from memory and she knew the lyrics to all the songs. She'd bought the ticket last week during intermission at the Saturday matinee.

If she hurried and didn't bother to dry her hair, she could certainly make it before the girls on stage lined up to do "Cell Block Tango". She sang softly to herself as she donned a pale pink sundress and tan sandals. *If you'd have been there, If you'd have seen it, I betcha you would have done the same.* Wrapping a floral print cashmere blend *Pashmina* around her shoulders, she turned out the lights and decided to take her car. She might even make it on time for Elliot's grand entrance.

CB

Elliot Scott stood in the shadows of the wings listening to lyrics. Waiting. He silently said familiar lines along with the lead actor who had the role of Billy Flynn, the dashing character he'd once played so many years ago on Broadway. He waited for the cue to bring his own supporting character on stage. Amos Hart - loyal, considerate, decent, humble, faithful Amos.

Maybe if he'd been cast in this role back then, he would have learned something which could have helped him be a better husband? Maybe the flamboyant character of Flynn had gotten under his skin? Sometimes actors had been known to take on the persona of the people they portray on stage every night. He wished he could use that as an excuse for what he did. What Morgan had convinced him was best for … She'd been at the matinee last Saturday. Came to congratulate him after his performance "even though you weren't one of the leads". She'd never been one for subtlety.

He heard his cue and putting on his hat, walked on the stage for his big number of the night.

Selina leaned over the balcony of the theatre watching Elliot shuffle across the stage singing his tale of woe. "You can look right through me, Walk right by me and never know I'm there."

She remembered the first time she'd seen him. Her friend Morgan had tickets for *A Streetcar Named Desire* at Trinity Square Repertory Company. The lead actor playing Stanley Kowalski had broken his foot and Elliot was the stand-in. His performance that evening had begun his rise in theater.

"That guy's a hunk," Morgan had whispered to her while he strutted around on stage in his tight black pants and white undershirt.

Back at the apartment, Selina had written in her journal: *Elliot Scott was mesmerizing from the moment he stepped onto the stage from the wings. Morgan used her connections to get us into the dressing room afterwards and introduced herself, making sure he knew her parents were major donors to the Rep Company. She asked him if he'd like to escort us out for a drink and he was more than happy to oblige. I couldn't take my eyes off him. He's the most gorgeous guy I've ever seen. Morgan told me she was going to have her parents host a party for the cast. She's set her sights on him and he doesn't stand a chance. They'll be engaged by the summer.*

A few months later, Selina found herself writing another entry: *Morgan's tired of poor Elliot. He doesn't have enough money to keep her interested and has been relegated to the old boyfriend scrap heap. She's pleased to have found herself someone famous and rich and has moved on to bigger and better things. She and Grazio will make a great couple. Elliot was much too good for her, in my lowly opinion.*

For Christmas, Morgan's mother Lenore gave Selina a subscription to the next season's performances at Trinity. Sitting in the front row, she became Elliot's biggest fan and sent him flowers after he received rave reviews for his role as Beauregard Decker, the socially inept cowboy in *Bus Stop* searching for his angel in a run-down diner.

Elliot showed up at her apartment one night wearing the Stetson hat from the play. They spent time getting to know each other better in the booth of a nearby cafe. At the end of the evening, he told her he'd found his angel and before the next semester she'd dropped out of college and followed him to Broadway. By then, she'd completely lost herself to him.

Once again, tonight, Selina found herself captivated by his performance. He was no longer cast in the lead role, but he brought the house down with his "Mr. Cellophane". Elliot still had it. She toyed with the idea of going to the cabaret in the bar after the performance hoping to see him, but decided, in the end, not to.

4

Let me sit here forever with bare things,
this coffee cup, this knife, this fork,
things in themselves, myself being myself.

-Virginia Woolf, *The Waves*

DETECTIVE CARL SULLIVAN HAD nicked himself shaving.
Dabbing at the tiny cut, he turned on the tap to rinse the drops of
blood from the bathroom sink. He was up early. He went into the kitchen
where he sat at the table reading the sports page. Freshly ground coffee
dripped into the carafe and cinnamon rolls were warming in the oven. He
knew the peace and solitude would not last once the aroma had wafted
through the living room and into the boys' bedroom.

The family dog, Max was the first to come bounding in followed closely
by eight-year-old Billy. Connor wandered in wearing only the top of his
pajamas and red leather cowboy boots.

"Good morning, you two. Hey, looks a mite drafty down there. Where's
your pants, Buddy?"

Connor ignored his father. He opened the refrigerator and stared up
at the carton of chocolate milk. Billy took it out and poured some into a
sippy cup for his little brother.

"Any idea where the bottoms could be?" Carl asked his eldest.

"I'll check the toilet," he volunteered, returning a few seconds later.
"Not there."

Jess arrived. "Good morning, family." She kissed her husband.
"Anything important happening in the world?"

"Red Sox are playing the Yankees tonight."

"Um, I thought we'd had this discussion before we got married and agreed baseball is a sport and sports are not news. They belong on the back pages dedicated to adult games and pastimes just before the comics and in the section aptly named Sports."

"Look," he held up the paper which she chose to ignore. "It's on the front page – with pictures, even. Somebody else must think it's worthy of being called news."

She sighed, pouring herself a mug of coffee. "What about the real news?"

"Let's see … they've released the name of the victim from that car accident in Narragansett." He turned the page to face her and pointed to the article. "Morgan Duckworth."

"Is your cousin Gerry assigned to the case?"

"I spoke with him yesterday and he says they're all working 24-7. It's not that large a police department in Narragansett, so everyone's going to be busy until they track down the driver. He called to ask for my advice."

"Have they found the vehicle?"

"Yup. And here's the weird thing. He told me she was hit by her own car – a silver *Alfa Romeo*."

"That's odd. Any suspects?"

"Nope."

"Was she married?"

"Yup. And now you're going to tell me the husband did it."

"You're the detective in the house. Don't you cops always look to the spouse first?"

"Only the wives." He ducked when she swatted at his head with the Rhode Islander section.

"But her husband couldn't have done it. Gerry told me that he's already dead."

"Well, I guess that gets him off the hook. Ummm, those rolls smell delicious."

Connor pointed to the oven and gaped at both of his parents expectantly.

"They'll be done in five minutes when the timer goes off. Why don't you go find your pajama bottoms?" his father suggested.

Connor shrugged his shoulders and left the kitchen.

"Do you have plans for today?" Jess asked.

"I told Billy he could decide. So, what ideas have you come up with?" He looked to his son.

"How about going to the aquarium in Mystic and then to the Seaport and then we can get chowder and clam cakes and eat on the beach?"

"Wow! That's a full day," his mother said.

"Or we can skip the Seaport and just go right to Moonstone. I like the beach best when most of the tourists are gone and we have it to ourselves."

The timer on the stove went off. Carl took the cookie tray from the oven and drizzled the white, creamy frosting onto the hot rolls, putting extra on Billy's. They were enjoying their breakfast when the three-year-old returned and placed his hands on his hips.

"Where's mine?" he looked at each of them.

"I think the real question is, 'Where are your pajamas?'" his father said handing him a bun.

"Don't like clothes," the naked child declared and sat in the middle of the floor licking off all the icing and then tearing apart small pieces of the dough to share with Max.

"You'd think he was being raised by wolves," Billy muttered.

"It certainly would appear that way," his father agreed, bending his head back to howl at the ceiling.

☙

Stewart and Kara Langley were still in their robes reading and enjoying steaming cups of lemon ginger tea.

"Doctor Morgan Duckworth," Stewart mumbled to himself.

"What about her?" his wife asked.

"The hit and run." He pointed to the article on the second page of the *Providence Journal.*

Kara leaned over to scan the article. "Ummm ... I'll have to visit Professor Hill at the crime lab and get the details."

"I thought you were taking some time off from solving murders, Detective Langley. Are you already tired of the daily routine of bringing up baby?" Stewart looked over the top of the paper to smile at her.

"I'm just curious. I used to be the first to know everything when I was on the force. Now, I'm just like every other bystander being kept in the dark."

Kara had turned her badge in at the end of May, deciding to spend more time with her daughter. Celia was lying on a quilted blanket looking at the ceiling and flailing her tiny hands up toward the sunlight beams streaming into the living room. At four months old, she was beginning to notice everything around her.

"I never get tired of watching her. She's growing up too fast for my liking."

"Sophia thinks she's extremely advanced for her age," Stewart put the Sudoku puzzle down and waved at the baby. "Look, I think she's waving back at me," he told his wife.

"And I think Celia's Auntie Sophia has you all brainwashed. She said, 'goo gaa gaa' the other day when they were babysitting, and Gino was convinced she was asking for the latest Lady Gaga album."

"I was wondering where that new CD came from," Stewart said.

"Ruth called and asked if I wanted to go to Moonstone for a picnic with her and Sophia later this afternoon. They were there last weekend after that big thunderstorm and she said it was gorgeous. Not crowded, no litter, and the water was warm and calm. I'm not much of a beach person, but Sophia told Ruth it would be good for Celia to feel the sand and dip her toes into the ocean. Before the cold weather seeps in."

"Now who's acting brain-washed?" Her husband took the loose-leaf binder entitled Baby Langley from the coffee table. Sophia had compiled resources on child development. Among them were articles on tactile stimulation. She'd placed sticker notes on the section devoted to encouraging infant neurological growth through maximum use of the five senses.

"I've read some of those, and I think she's on to something. After all, Sophia's a pediatric nurse. She does have some expertise on the subject."

"I'd think twice before encouraging her," Stewart warned. "Gino says we should get Celia a pet or two or three. He's suggesting something furry, something slimy, and something scaly. To go along with the tactile stimulation theme. I suggested they just take her to Roger Williams Park once a week and let her pet the animals there."

"Grrrrr."

"Did you hear? She made an animal noise! She obviously likes the idea of a trip to the zoo," Stewart declared.

Kara picked up her daughter and held her close, kissing her forehead. "And I think she's just a baby being a baby who's telling us she's hungry."

ϗ

"If you're still hungry, I can make you another omelet," Ruth offered taking the last slice of bacon from the platter.

Rick didn't answer her. His attention was elsewhere. "I know this person - Dr. Morgan Duckworth, Yvonne's old GP." He put down the newspaper and stared at his empty plate.

"She treated Yvonne?"

"No, she didn't."

"But you just said she was her doctor."

"I'd hardly call her a doctor. Sophia refers to her as 'The Quack' and I pretty much agree with her assessment of the woman. Duckworth was one of those misinformed, condescending physicians who determined mammograms were not necessary for young women if there was no history of cancer in the family. It was why Yvonne was not diagnosed earlier." Rick got up and took the paper outside to sit on the patio.

Ruth brought him a fresh cup of coffee. She could hear her cell phone ringing and went into the house to search for it. She interrupted the sound of Sophia's voice leaving a voice mail.

"I called to see if you still wanted to go to Moonstone today. I have something important to …"

"Hey, it's me. Sorry. It took me a while to track down my phone. And yes, I do want to go to the beach. Kara and Celia will be joining us."

"Great, I'll pick you all up around two at your place. Give Rick a hug for me. Bye."

"Wait. You said you had something important to tell me," Ruth reminded her.

"I'll tell you this afternoon." She hung up.

Ruth returned to the patio to find her husband watching an emerald-throated hummingbird flit around the feeder.

"He should be flying south by now," Rick said.

The little creature chirped and whirred, stopping intermittently for brief sips.

"It's been warm, so maybe he decided to stick around for another week," she said. "That was Sophia. We're going to the beach."

"Did she call to remind me Gino was coming over to watch the game?" Rick asked.

"She didn't mention it, but she hinted that she had some important news."

"What news?"

"I'm not sure. She was being coy and said she'd tell me later. Just Sophia being Sophia." Ruth bent down to give him a hug.

ଓ

5

The beach is not a place to work; to read, write, or think.

- Anne Morrow Lindbergh, *Gift from the Sea*

THE THREE FRIENDS SET up their own little space on the beach using blankets and towels to mark their territory next to the crab pond.

"When we were kids, my parents brought my brother, my sister, and me here and we always staked out our place around the pond. My dad would give us each a length of string, a hook, and some stale bread to catch crabs." Kara shared her memories with her friends. "We never kept them. We'd just throw them back in." She placed Celia's baby carrier under a brightly striped umbrella in the middle of it all facing out to sea so she could look to the waves and at the people walking along the shore.

A breeze picked up the ends of the towels and Sophia collected rocks to anchor the edges in place. She brought one of the smaller grey stones to the baby and guided her tiny fingers along the hard-rounded surface.

"Moonstone. Oooooh. Smoooth. Pretty moonstone, Celia."

The baby seemed to be concentrating on the geology lesson, her brow furrowed as she patted the object Sophia held out to her. "Moo buh guh ghu."

"See she knows exactly what I'm saying," Sophia rose. "I'm going to find some shells for her. Without jagged edges." She skipped off toward the shoreline.

"Well, it would appear you are raising a baby Einstein," Ruth chuckled when their friend was out of earshot.

"She's always smiling and she's healthy. That's all I care about for the time being. I certainly don't need a precocious child at my age. A healthy, happy baby is fine with me."

Sophia returned placing a handful of weathered sea glass, rocks, and shells at Celia's feet and began putting them in order according to size. "Gifts from the sea, little one." The baby wiggled her legs and laughed. Her toes brushed one of the shells off the blanket. "Did you see how far that shell went? A future World Cup soccer player. Another Megan Rapinoe," Sophia proudly announced.

"No doubt about it," her mother conceded.

"So, when are you going to tell us this important piece of information?" Ruth asked.

They waited while Sophia made herself comfortable and opened a bottle of cold water. She took a long swig before sharing her news. "Did you read the article about the woman who was killed in the hit and run ?"

"Morgan Duckworth," Kara offered.

"Better known as 'The Quack'," Sophia declared. "And do you know why?"

Kara shook her head but Ruth said, "Rick told me she was Yvonne's doctor. The one who failed to diagnose her cancer because she didn't believe in mammograms for younger women."

"Oh, no. What kind of doctor thinks that way in this day and age?" Kara looked at her two friends.

"A Quack!" Sophia informed them. "And Evie wasn't the only one she failed to diagnose. The Medical Board suspended her license after a class action suit was brought against her regarding prostate cancer patients who'd been getting regular check-ups and tests done but she never bothered to tell them the PSA levels on their blood tests were doubling. Come to find out, many of the men didn't even know what a prostate-specific antigen level was until it was too late and their cancers had metastasized."

"Why did she bother to run the tests if she had no intention of discussing results with her patients?" Ruth curiosity was piqued.

"I'm told it's more common than you'd think. Doctors not understanding tests or how important it is to go over them with patients. And she neglected to do anything about a man with blood in his urine. He died of bladder cancer. And it wasn't just cancer patients who took her to court. She apparently didn't believe in prescribing antibiotics for Lyme disease which she'd first misdiagnosed to be *fibromyalgia*. Her solution was bed rest."

Kara was astonished. "How long did she get away with such incompetence?"

"It took years for them to catch up with her. Evie once confided in me that Morgan was a brilliant student but never should have been awarded a degree involving working with human beings. Of course, her parents were well connected and wealthy. I'm talking huge donations and funding hospital wings rich. Money - always the great manipulator."

"Did you ever work with her, Sophia?" Ruth asked.

"She was at a hospital in New York City where I was assigned when I was studying for my nursing degree. I met Yvonne at a workshop at the hospital when she was part of a panel on breast cancer. She'd been Morgan's patient but changed to an oncologist when she found she had late stage cancer which had gone undetected. Yvonne was the one who introduced me to Rick and later on I met Gino at Rick's art gallery."

"Well, that's interesting," Kara said but she could tell by the way Sophia looked at them the story wasn't over. "Besides her connection to Yvonne and Rick and her gross incompetence, what else do you know about Morgan Duckworth?"

"When her father died, she returned to the family's estate on Ocean Road. By the time she came back to Rhode Island, she wasn't practicing anymore. She started an herbal remedy business in Narragansett. I've been in there a few times. She always asks for Rick."

Ruth looked questioningly at her friend. "Why would she ask about Rick?"

"Maybe because he kept friendly with her mother, Lenore?"

"Sophia, why do I have a feeling you're not giving me the whole story? What else is there about this I should know?"

"Ummm ... let's just say in New York she ran around with the smart set and had money to burn. She was an avid arts patron, and she liked hanging around Rick's gallery looking for up-and-coming artists she could ... ummmm ... sponsor. It was before Yvonne's illness."

"Didn't Morgan have a husband?"

"Oh, she had lots of husbands, and they were all married to other women."

"How did Yvonne feel about Morgan being Rick's *avid* patron?"

"Oh, Evie had nothing to worry about. Rick's as faithful as they come. He was quite good at keeping Morgan in her place which made her even more avid, if you get my gist."

"I'm definitely getting your gist. Go on."

Sophia looked at Ruth. "You know that woman who was building the sandcastle last week?"

"What about her?" Ruth was curious.

"Well, she was married to Elliot Scott. Morgan broke up their marriage. Small world, huh?"

"Rick mentioned Selina had been married to Scott. But he didn't say anything about a break-up," Ruth said.

"What else do you know?" Kara asked.

"Nothing much. Morgan Duckworth betrayed Yvonne, destroyed Selina and Elliot's marriage, her husband supposedly fell into the sea at Hazard's Rock, and now she's dead. End of story."

"Seems to me the story has a long way to go. Someone killed her and from what you've just told us, there are plenty of people with strong motives for murder," Kara declared.

"Buh, Buh, moo, moo." The baby joined in on the conversation.

"I think Celia wants her mother to put her big girl detective pants back on and figure it all out," Sophia said, picking up her niece and walking toward the waves lapping onto the shore. "Come on little girl, let's get your cute tootsies wet."

"Look Connor, it's Celia!" Billy grabbed his little brother's hand and ran to the baby who was watching the three women engrossed in crafting a sandcastle with plastic beach pails. Jess and Carl followed after them picking up the trail of towels and beach toys their sons had dropped in their excitement.

"Celia! Look, it's me. It's me, Connor!" He jumped up and down, dancing in front of them and knocking over one side of the castle as he twirled around to get the baby's attention. She rewarded him with laughter, and he gave her a gentle kiss on the top of her head. Billy immediately began rebuilding the wall.

Carl spread out their blanket and Jess asked if anyone was hungry. "We have plenty." She began unpacking bags and taking food from the cooler as they settled in for a picnic while the boys played at chasing seagulls up and down the beach.

"Well, looks like you're finally getting some time off. It's good to see you out of the office." Kara said to her old partner.

"I'm actually finishing up a two-week vacation," Carl said.

"You've got a nice tan," Sophia offered.

"That's from standing on a ladder in the hot sun," he told her. The house now has a fresh coat of paint and the garage has been cleaned out. After twenty trips to the land fill, I'm happy to announce, we have a place to start storing another ten years of junk. But for now, I don't have to park my car on the street."

"Yup, he's dying for this vacation to end so he can get some well-earned rest." Jess handed her husband another clam cake and a Del's Lemonade.

"At least things have been quiet in South Kingstown. Although it looks like the Narragansett police have a murder to investigate," Ruth said.

"Yeah, it's a strange one. I'll probably learn more when I get back to work. My cousin Gerry's a cop in Narragansett. He sometimes calls to ask me about any connections his cases have in South Kingstown. He called to see if I knew anything about one of the suspects who lives here in town. I didn't recognize the name."

"Sophia was telling us that she and Rick knew Morgan Duckworth in New York. Rick's first wife, Evie, was her patient." Kara waited for Carl to offer more information.

"Small world. The woman they brought in for questioning also had been a patient of Dr. Duckworth," he said.

"They think the hit and run driver might be a woman?" Sophia was surprised.

"Did your cousin have any more info?" Kara asked.

"They're delving into the background, but it would appear Duckworth stole this person's husband."

"If every woman who stole someone's husband was murdered, there'd be a lot of dead bodies lying around," Sophia announced.

"There's more to the story. The suspect also had sued Duckworth for malpractice. The trial was ugly with accusations the good doctor had wanted the patient dead so she could marry the husband."

"Sounds like a great idea for a best-seller," Ruth said. "How did it end?"

"Dr. Duckworth's husband apparently committed suicide, she lost her license and closed her practice, the suspect's marriage broke up, and no one lived happily ever after."

"When did this all happen?" Kara asked.

"About nine years ago."

"A long time to hold a grudge," Jess commented

"Conventional wisdom has it that revenge is a dish best served cold," Ruth said and, although she had a pretty good idea who the person was, she asked, "Did Gerry give you the name of the suspect?"

"She's a local artist - a sculptor. Selina Borelli."

After everyone had eaten, Kara and Carl stayed behind with Celia while the others went off on an adventure.

"So what have you found out so far about the accident?" Kara asked.

"Not much more than what's been in the papers. She was run down by her own car.

Gerry says they came across the car when they went to the house after they traced the ID on the body. She wasn't discovered until the next morning. A woman called it in. When the cops went to the address on Ocean Road, they found the front door unlocked. Nobody was in the house, but two dogs were running around the property. They belonged to the victim. The car was in an old garage at the end of the gravel driveway."

"No one was home? Did she live alone?"

"Evidently. But, according to her mother, she had occasional guests during the summer months. No one was visiting at the time of the accident."

"I heard the house belonged to her parents. Does her mother still live there?"

"Mrs. Duckworth still owns the estate and the cars although Morgan has total use of it all. The mother has living quarters on the third floor where she stays from time to time. She had the nursery redone into an apartment for herself when her daughter returned to Rhode Island but for all intents and purposes, she moved out of the house two years ago. She said she wanted a smaller place where she could be with friends. She belongs to a bridge club at Sea View, the upscale retirement community where she lives."

"How did she take the news about her daughter?"

"My cousin said the mother was quite calm about the whole thing. It could have been due to the fact she'd been drinking before the police arrived. She didn't say much. He got the feeling, from the little she did say and her total lack of emotion given the news of her daughter's death, that they may have been estranged. I advised Gerry to get a copy of any wills and look for some motivation there. And they've been calling on friends and acquaintances of the deceased and are beginning to look into her former patients. I think that's where they'll find some persons of interest, if they ask the right questions."

"Has the crime lab given them any leads from the evidence they collected?" Kara was beginning to be interested in this case.

"Gerry didn't say. They've called in all their manpower to work on the interrogations and statements, hoping they'll point in the right direction."

"Do you think he'd mind if I looked over the evidence at the lab and spoke with Professor Hill?"

"I don't think he'd mind at all but you could ask him yourself, if you'd like. I'm having a Labor Day barbeque at my place and you're invited. It'll just be family and I'm sure Connor would love it if Celia were there. Maybe it would distract him enough to keep his clothes on for a few hours."

"We'll be there. Stewart's been looking for a reason to make his famous end of summer dish."

"Sounds interesting. What's in it?"

"You don't want to know," she said. "He calls it his 'Don't Ask, Don't Tell - End of Summer, Clean out the Gardens, Blue Plate Extraordinaire'."

"Well, I'll make sure there'll be plenty of hot dogs, clam cakes and chowder then."

෴

6

Perhaps this is the most important thing for me
to take back from the beach – living:
Simply the memory that each cycle of the tide is valid;
each cycle of the wave is valid; each cycle of a relationship is valid.

-Anne Morrow Lindbergh, *Gift from the Sea*

WHEN RUTH ARRIVED HOME, Rick was in the laundry room putting clothes into the washing machine. "Did you have a pleasant afternoon at the beach?"

Ruth handed him her beach towel and bathing suit to add to the wash. "Yes, it was an interesting day on many levels."

"I made some Margueritas. I'll bring them out to the patio and you can tell me all about it."

Ruth hesitated to share what she'd learned about Selina Borelli and Morgan Duckworth. She didn't want to open up old wounds, but she wanted her husband to know what was happening with these people from his past. She opted, fnally, to tell him about the fun she'd had with her friends on the beach.

"After we made sandcastles, Celia fell asleep. Carl and Kara talked shop and Jess, Sophia, and I took the boys for a walk. At one point, Connor went running into the water and came out without his swim trunks. Jess took it in stride, as usual. Billy announced that Connor had spent a lot of time this summer naked. It appears his little brother finds clothes confining. Billy's totally disgusted and is thinking of moving to Canada – without his brother." They both laughed at the recent antics of their favorite siblings.

"Then Moonstone Beach is the perfect place for Connor. They should take him up to the nudist section and he can join in the topless volleyball game," Rick suggested.

"That's exactly what Jess said, and Billy threatened to run into the dunes with the piping clovers and stay there until the cops came to arrest him for trespassing into the nesting area."

"It sounds like we should invite Jess over for Margueritas, with extra tequila." Rick went in to the fridge and brought back the pitcher to top off his wife's drink.

"Sophia snapped lots of pictures and is starting another book. The first chapter is entitled 'Celia's First Trip to the Ocean'."

"If this is just a regular day in the life of her niece, can you imagine what the holidays are going to be like? The potential chapter titles are infinite," Rick declared.

"She let me in on a secret. Gino's planning a surprise for this week. The title of the next chapter might be called 'Celia Visits a Pet Store'. I'm not sure whether I should give Kara a heads up."

"Sometimes it's better to just step back and let things take their course," Rick advised. "I've been meaning to ask how you think Kara is doing. Does she miss work?"

"It's funny you should say that. Carl was there and he and Kara were talking about the Duckworth hit and run case. On the way home, Kara told me he had some inside information from his cousin who's on the Narragansett police force." She waited to see how Rick would react.

"What did he have to say?"

"They have a few suspects."

"I imagine there are a number of people who would like to see Morgan dead."

Ruth was surprised at the sudden tension in her husband's voice. "Yes, I surmised that. From some of the things Carl related, the woman had serious issues with the people in her life."

"'Do no harm.' It's part of the Hippocratic Oath. Morgan caused a lot of harm to both patients and friends," Rick stated.

"I should tell you, they've been interviewing patients Morgan misdiagnosed. One of the prime suspects appears to be Selina Borelli."

"Ridiculous! Lena wouldn't hurt anyone. She was always kind and vulnerable in the years I knew her. Fragile even. If she had it in her to kill Morgan, she would have done it then, not ten years later, for God's sake. That's like declaring I'm a prime suspect. I had just as much cause as Lena to want Morgan Duckworth dead. Hell, I had more reason – Yvonne died because of that woman's stupidity – her incompetence. And I watched her suffer all those years. They should be knocking on my door, not Selina's." He finished his drink and refilled his glass.

Rick had never spoken much about the time in his life when he'd brought his wife home to be with her family in Rhode Island. He remained in South Kingstown after her death and then his brother and his wife had moved to get away from the city and be closer to him. Until he'd met Ruth, Gino and Sophia were the only ones he'd spent much time with. He'd sold his New York gallery, but continued working; taking photographs, gaining a name for himself with the small exhibits he chose to enter.

He sometimes drove the late shift for the local cab company and one evening, when Ruth had returned by train from Boston, they met by chance. Her car, which was parked in the Kingston Station lot, refused to start. He had just dropped off a fare and noticed her looking under the hood of her old Volkswagen Bug.

"Can I be of help?"

"Thanks, I've just called triple A. They'll be here any minute."

He looked under the hood for himself, furrowed his brow, and shook his head. "I'm sorry to inform you I know absolutely nothing about engines. I'll just wait here in case you need a ride." They introduced themselves and chatted until the pick-up truck arrived. The car had to be towed to a local garage and he took her duffel bag and threw it into the trunk of the cab.

"Where to?" he asked as she settled into the passenger seat.

"It's not very far. Just up a ways on South Road." When she got out, he wouldn't accept the money she'd offered.

"If your car is in the shop, I can give you a ride when you need one." He handed her his business card. "No charge."

"I teach at the college and it's a short walk from here to the campus, but thanks for the offer."

"You're a professor at URI? I have an exhibit in the Fine Arts Building. I'm a photographer. I've been teaching there part time. Maybe I'll see you around?" He watched her until she was safely inside her house. She waved at him from the doorway.

On the following Friday, she strolled across the quadrangle from her office to an exhibit room in Fine Arts. She waited on a bench surrounded by his photographs of the familiar places in South County. She felt safe. He found her there and sat next to her. It was the beginning of their courtship. She laughed later on when she spoke about those first few weeks. "The old maid and the handsome widower" was how she described it to her best friend Kara who agreed it might do well for the title of a romance book, should Ruth ever choose to venture into that genre. They'd married on Christmas Day, a year later, and though they shared many things about their lives, the time when Evie was dying was a dark period he had yet to speak of and Ruth was wise enough to respect that.

"It couldn't have been easy for you and Yvonne."

"It was terrible for everyone, especially her mother and father. Not just the cancer. It was the betrayal. Yvonne's parents worked for the Duckworth's. Mr. Ferrelli was their gardener and Mrs. Ferrelli cooked. The girls spent all of their days together. Evie told me it was where she learned to draw. They set up easels and painted pictures of all the flowers in the yard and the cliffs and the ocean."

"The Duckworths were generous. They paid for Yvonne to go to RISD. They knew how talented she was. Morgan, of course, went to Brown – to med school, graduated, started her practice, and married a Spanish guy who was famous and even richer than her parents. Yvonne didn't see much of her then, even though she was working in New York. The social circles they inhabited were miles apart.

"A few years after Yvonne and I got married, we decided to start a family. Something was wrong. She went to Morgan who put her on health drinks and vitamins, and told her to lose some weight. She neglected to do any tests to find out the cause of the problem. So the cancer went undetected and, as you know, I brought Evie back to Rhode Island to be with her family. When she died, Mrs. Duckworth, Lenore, sent a gigantic bouquet of camellias, her favorite flowers. And she came to the funeral.

I saw her in the back pew." He shook his head and held out his hand to Ruth who clasped it into her own.

"And how does Selina fit into all of this?" Ruth asked.

"She was friends with Yvonne. They went to RISD and shared an apartment on the East Side of Providence. Evie introduced Selina to Morgan and the three of them spent a lot of time together during college. They traveled to New York on the weekends and stayed at the Duckworth's apartment in Manhattan. Morgan was dating Elliot Scott, a young actor just getting his start at Trinity Rep. She had a lot of boyfriends, so it wasn't a big deal when they broke up and Elliot started seeing Selina. They married and at first, lived a charmed life. She became a sought-after artist and he became famous. Everyone wanted to be seen with them and they were at the top of the A-list. Their days and nights became a whirlwind of parties and special events."

"Sounds like a fairytale."

"A tale straight out of Grimm. Evil witches, lethal concoctions, sudden death, innocent victims. Lena's sculptures were being commissioned and she was traveling all over the world. Meanwhile, Elliot was having his own taste of success. He received a Tony nomination for his portrayal of Billy Flynn in *Chicago*. Morgan became interested in him again and at the same time, Lena took ill. She began losing weight. She was exhausted. Morgan prescribed a special diet and gave her injections of Vitamin B. One night, Elliot brought her to the hospital. She was in a lot of pain. She was rushed into surgery and it was found she had cancer. She almost died. Morgan had missed the symptoms."

"Carl mentioned other cases of malpractice," Ruth said.

"There were pending lawsuits against Morgan from patients she'd misdiagnosed. Grazio Lucresta, her husband, accused her of cheating on him with Scott. He was a big, stocky guy. His face was scarred from a bike accident. From what I remember, he wasn't very attractive, and he never smiled. But he was a well-known artist. Had money. A painter with a reputation for having a mercurial personality. He'd lost a lot of his investments in the recession. Was a heavy drinker and became increasingly erratic and unstable when he found out Morgan was divorcing him. His ego didn't take well to rejection. She had a restraining order out on him at one point. They separated and she returned to Narragansett for her father's funeral. I spoke with Grazio at the memorial service for Mr. Duckworth. Strangely enough, he showed up unexpectedly with Selina. They made quite the entrance. Morgan was infuriated. They were in the process of finalizing the divorce papers when he disappeared. He went out for a walk and a neighbor reported him standing on the edge of the rocks at Hazard Avenue. His body was never found."

"So much tragedy touching everyone," Ruth said.

"Morgan Duckworth was a toxic person. I sometimes wonder if she ever had a healthy relationship with anyone in her life."

"What about her parents?"

"Although her father adored her, I always felt there were underlying problems, especially with her mother. Nice lady. I've kept in touch with Lenore over the years. She's come to some of my exhibits and bought some of my work." He poured himself another drink. "Morgan left a lot of destruction in her wake. Now can you understand why I said there are a lot of people who would want her dead?"

Ruth had to agree. Dr. Morgan Duckworth certainly must have amassed quite a few enemies in her lifetime. And one of them had seen to it she'd ultimately met a terribly violent end.

ଔ

7

Tell me the story
About how the sun loved the moon so much
That she died every night
Just to let him breathe

- Hanako Ishii

SELINA SAT IN HER car in the parking lot of the Narragansett police station after giving her statement. There was no point in denying there'd been bad blood between Morgan and her. She related the story of their past history, leaving nothing out – even the fact they'd recently had words. For the interview, she wore a low-cut t-shirt and her scar was visible.

The previous night she'd written in her journal: *They'll try to find evidence I killed Morgan. I have a motive and no alibi. I've welcomed this time alone with just myself and the sea. But, solitude has its drawbacks. No one to bear witness to my comings and goings. I told them my life has changed. I'm older, wiser, less ambitious, less naïve, less trusting. Lessons well learned. Thank you for that, Morgan, my old friend.*

Elliot looked at his caller ID, took a deep breath and picked up on the third ring. "Selina. How are you? I've been wanting to see you while I was here in South County. Did you get my messages?"

"I've been better, Elliot. I'm sorry I didn't get back to you until now."

"It's good to hear your voice. I was hoping I could talk to you before I returned to New York."

"Do you have a show coming up?"

"No. Sunny… my agent, has lined up a few appointments, but I'm biding my time. I actually like summer stock. It's work and vacation all rolled into one. This is the first time I've been hired to perform at Theatre-By-the-Sea. I saw they were doing my old show and got Sunny to arrange an audition. Lots of memories." He gave a half-hearted laugh.

"I was calling to see if we might get together." She held her breath.

"I'd love to meet, Selina. Maybe you could come by this afternoon? There's a little bistro at the theater. We could do lunch."

She exhaled. "That would be nice. I'll see you there around two."

She well understood the irony of him acting in a production of *Chicago* in Matunuck. She always identified that production as the one marking the beginning of the end of their relationship. In her twenties, she realized when she read her journal, most of the entries centered around him. *Elliot Scott is the most gorgeous, talented man I've ever met.* When she found him in Morgan's arms, the day their marriage ended, she'd scrawled on the page: *Betrayal – the vilest, ugliest of all sins. In a friend. In a husband.* Many times she'd looked back on those days, as she opened the journal to the entry where tears had bled the heartbreaking words into the wrinkled paper.

Their marriage had started out perfectly. It encompassed a time in their lives when they'd both reached pinnacles in their careers. Her art was in demand and her husband was receiving the recognition he'd worked so hard for over the years. Cast as Billy Flynn, the slick, winning lawyer who specialized in trials involving cold-hearted, murderous wives, the role gave Scott a chance to showcase all of his talents; singing, dancing, acting.

Selina returned from an exhibit in London to support him on his rise to fame. She'd been exhausted from the work and the constant travel and on the edge of a breakdown. They decided it would be best for her to take a hiatus and spend some time basking in the limelight together. He'd been uncomfortable with the notoriety his new stardom was bringing and was glad to have her by his side to keep the female fans at bay.

Then there was Morgan. Elliot had dated her for a few months but in the end, he'd married Selina. The women were as different as night and day and he often wondered what he'd ever seen in Morgan. She was self-absorbed, callous, class-conscious, materialistic, and calculating. Selina was kind, patient, and the gentlest person he'd ever met. In spite of knowing all of this, in spite of having everything he could have possibly dreamed, he'd cast it all away.

Selina became ill and was hospitalized. During the whole terrible time, Morgan had been there for him. His wife hadn't told him she'd gone to Morgan when she first felt ill and it was Morgan who had failed to diagnose her cancer. At the time, Selina had been in denial. She'd felt a strange loyalty toward her old friend. It wasn't until much later, when the tabloids ran a front page spread detailing how this well-known artist's doctor and her husband were an item, that she told him the whole story. But it was too late to salvage their marriage. She hired a lawyer, divorced Elliot, and sued Morgan.

Selina eventually returned to Rhode Island and lived a quiet life in South County, continuing to do her art, specializing in mostly smaller pieces, and stone sculptures which were eagerly bought by influential clients with discrete taste. She had a studio in Wickford in an old mill with other artists, but she'd kept to herself, lacking the trust it would take to build new friendships or to renew the old. And she found she'd become anxious and filled with conflicting feelings. She just didn't have the strength left to even try.

Elliot placed his phone on the bureau. He'd been so happy to hear Selina's voice. He stuffed the clothes he was preparing to pack into a suitcase and threw it under the bed. He stashed the dirty dishes into the dishwasher and straightened the movie magazines on the coffee table. Maybe she'd come home with him after lunch. Maybe they could be friends again. Maybe he could undo it all now that Morgan was finally out of their lives. He closed his eyes and thought about the idyllic life they'd once had. And now they were meeting as friends. Friends who'd been separated by time and circumstance. He wondered if she would be the same as he remembered – his sweet, adoring wife. He wondered if the years had changed her.

She walked into the café and looked around until she caught sight of him. He had to stop himself from sobbing at the sight of her and at the immensity of what he'd lost. Elliot stood up as she moved toward the table. In that moment, the silence between them was so deafening, not even the sound of the waves crashing on the beach outside could be heard in the room.

She hesitated a second, then gave him a hug. They sat down and looked at the menu, neither caring about what they would order. Over a bottle of wine, they spoke of happier times and brought each other up to date on what their lives had now become.

After lunch they walked on the beach and the present insinuated itself like a tidal wave between the screeching of the seagulls circling overhead.

"Elliot, I think I need help. I have no one else to turn to. I have no family. No friends. Morgan is dead. I've been brought in for questioning and I'm sure I'll be arrested for her murder. I don't know where else to go."

"No one could possibly believe you're capable of killing Morgan. These people don't know you. There are plenty of others with more reason than you. They should look into the other patients who sued her for malpractice. The information is there."

Selina began to cry. He put his arms around her, and she rested her head on his chest.

"I'll contact the police myself if I have to and explain about her history of incompetence. I could give them a list of people who had plenty of reason to kill her. It's all right, Selina. Tell me what you want me to do. I'll help you."

She looked up at him. "I know you will. I just need someone to talk to who understands what went on so many years ago when we were in New York where all of this started."

"I always felt it began long before that, when Morgan was young. She used to tell me stories about her parents and how they favored her sister."

"She spoke to me about Angela once. She briefly told me what had happened without going into specifics and quickly ended the conversation by saying she preferred being an only child," Selina said.

"She was only seven when her sister died. She told me her parents soon replaced Angela with Yvonne. They'd hired Mr. and Mrs. Ferrelli and paid them to bring their daughter with them as a companion for Morgan. She had a difficult time making friends because after the death of her sister, she became introverted. Yvonne seemed to be a calming influence and the situation worked well for everyone."

"I don't think Yvonne knew she was there as paid help. At least she never mentioned it to me. Exactly what did she tell you happened to the child?"

"It seems she fell from the third-floor balcony off the nursery. The door had been left open. Lenore told the police that Morgan carried Angela into the house. The nanny found her wrapping bandages around the bruises. The child was dead, but Morgan was talking to her as if she were still alive. I think the problems began then. The Duckworths hired the best psychologists, but the damage was deep. Her mother always felt if her daughter became a doctor and helped others to mend, she would finally be whole again. But we know that didn't happen."

"Morgan shared all of this with you?"

"It's what we talked about while you were in the hospital. I thought you were going to die. She said she understood what it was like to lose someone you loved deeply. It's what drew us closer together. I'm sorry, Selina. I didn't mean for all of that to happen. If I could just go back and change it, I would."

"Why didn't you marry her when Grazio died?"

"Ah, another name from our past. I remember he was enthralled with you and I never understood why he married Morgan."

"He asked me. He showed up one night with an immense sapphire ring. He was crushed when I said no. By that time, I knew I was in love with you. I always felt he became engaged to Morgan to make me jealous."

"And Morgan was happy to trade me in for someone richer and more famous from what I remember."

"So, why didn't you marry her when Grazio died?"

"His body was never found. It took time to declare him dead. It gave me enough time to realize I wasn't in love with her."

"I despised her for what she did to me – to us. You'd think I could forgive a dead woman. But I can't. I'm relieved she's gone. I'm not the docile Selina everyone thinks they know. Inside I'm angry and calloused. I've nurtured the incubus for such a long time, it's devoured the person I once was."

"I don't believe it. I see the same beautiful woman I married and loved for all those years."

"That woman doesn't exist. The police can sense what I'm really thinking. It's why they called me in for questioning. I know they're gathering evidence. I have no alibi. I'm afraid to tell them about ...."

"What do you mean, Selina? Do you know something? If you know something, you have to tell them. You could be in danger."

"In my heart I wanted her dead, Elliot. Every morning, when I woke up and began my day, I wanted her to be gone. And now she is. I have no alibi. It's just a matter of time before I'm arrested. I don't think I can live in a cage. I spent so much time in that hospital. I need to be near the ocean and to breathe fresh air." She walked toward the sound of the waves and on to the beach.

He caught up with her and took her by the hand. "What do you want me to do?"

"I need somebody to believe in me when I say I didn't kill her."

Before she went to bed, she wrote in her journal: *I can finally breathe again. Elliot has faith in me. He won't let them lock me away. It felt like old times when it was just the two of us. We were golden then. I can trust him to protect me. I feel safe. For the first time in years, I can fall asleep knowing someone loves me.*

☙

8

*It's a curious fact that novelists have a way of making us believe
that luncheon parties are invariably memorable
for something very witty that was said,
or for something very wise that was done.
But they seldom spare a word for what was eaten.*

-Virginia Woolf, *A Room of One's Own*

THE FIRST WEEKEND IN September signaled the official end of summer in South County. Children would be going back to school. Bulk mail flyers were filled with ads for sales. Beaches would finally be cleared of tourists caught in traffic jams on Rte.95 in their rush to return to everyday jobs and everyday lives. Roads leading to the university would be filled with cars of returning students for the fall semester. And then the quiet could begin to settle in as leaves turned from green to golden shades to reds and then to caramel colored tans before the branches bared all, preparing for the winter's white frost.

A Labor Day barbeque was the requisite way for many to celebrate the seasonal transition. Local markets stocked up on hamburgers, hot dogs, potato salad, chips, and rolls and the liquor stores enjoyed a surge in beer sales. The Sullivan family tradition meant they would take turns hosting a cookout and this year the party was at Carl's house on Sunday afternoon, since he'd be working on Monday.

When the Langleys arrived, the celebration was in full swing. They cautiously worked their way past a raucous volleyball game on the front lawn around to the back yard.

Connor came running toward them announcing to everyone, "Celia's here. My friend Celia's here!" Carl waved to them from his post at the grill and Jess took Stewart's homemade casserole to the serving table on the patio.

They settled into lawn chairs under a tall oak where Carl had built a tree house for the boys. Connor got his brother to climb up the ladder and fetch a book for him. He then went into the house to return with his favorite blanket, spreading it on the ground. Kara placed the baby carrier next to him and he began to explain to his friend why she was too young to eat a hot dog.

"When you get your baby teeth, Celia, you should eat lots of vegetables. Carrots, and peas, and squash. Your mommy can mash them up for you." He looked at Kara and she nodded in agreement. He opened the book. "This is about a baby pitcher plant. Pitcher plants eat bugs. But this one decides he's not going to kill bugs. He's going to follow his heart and be a vegetarian. That means he's just going to eat vegetables." He opened the first page for her and began to read aloud.

"That's amazing. He's only three. And Sophia thinks Celia is a genius!" Stuart exclaimed.

"How long has he been reading?" Kara asked Carl who had brought his cousin Gerry over to introduce to Kara.

"Don't be too impressed. The book comes with a CD. He's listened to it so often, he knows the whole story by heart. This is my cousin Gerry. He's one of the Narragansett cops assigned to the hit-and-run investigation. I told him you've been doing some consulting and working with the forensics people at the state lab."

Stuart got up to give Gerry his seat. "Could you use some help with the food?" he asked hopefully.

"Definitely. I think I may have an extra apron around somewhere for a chef of your caliber."

Although Stuart taught science at the college, his real passion was concocting original recipes in his kitchen. Recipes with ingredients only an astrophysicist would think of. Carl gave Kara a wink as they walked away toward the grill.

"It's great to finally meet you. Carl has sung your praises for years. He really misses having you as a partner." Gerry sat down.

"He and the rest of the team are doing a great job without me and I can always help him as a consultant or with my work in the forensics lab."

"That's what I wanted to talk to you about. I'm pretty new to this detective role and I was hoping I could go to you if I needed some help with this murder investigation. I spoke with my captain and he has a lot of respect for you. Professor Hill told him you'd be working together on some of the evidence we sent to the lab. The captain asked me if I thought you might be available as a consultant. I said I'd mention it to you."

"I'll certainly do whatever I can to help with the investigation."

"That's great. As Carl told you, there's overlap. Some of the people we've been questioning are from South Kingstown. We'll be bringing them in for further questions. A guy called me with names of patients who may have been holding a grudge against the doctor. We've been busy following up on leads. Morgan's mother is an interesting character."

"In what way?"

"When we went to her condo at Sea View Estates to tell her about her daughter's death, she was sitting on the patio adjacent to the dining room wearing rhinestone studded sun glasses, and all bundled up in a mink jacket, ivory satin gloves, and a silk scarf. It's quite a ritzy place. Must cost a pretty penny. We gave her the bad news and she said she was prepared to go with us to identify the body. I told her it might not be necessary for her to go to the morgue and asked if there were any discerning birthmarks. She described, in detail, a dragonfly tattoo we could find on her daughter's left shoulder and then proceeded to tell us how Morgan had gotten it without permission when she was a teenager. The story went on for quite a while. When it appeared she was finished, I showed her a photo and she said 'Yes, that's my daughter.' And quickly gave it back to me like it had burnt her fingers."

He took the victim's photo from his wallet and handed it to Kara.

"Her face doesn't seem to have been affected."

"We were able to get the picture because, although the body had been severely injured, the killer only drove the car over her legs and torso."

"Do you think Mrs. Duckworth was in shock? Her reaction seems quite out of the ordinary for a mother receiving such horrific news."

"I don't know what to make of it. She swallowed some pills with water, but she might have been tipsy because she took a small bell from her coat pocket and rang it. A waiter came out and she told him to bring her another Bloody Mary and another dish of prawns. I'm planning on returning to speak with her. I was wondering if you would go with me. Carl says you're the best when it comes to asking the right questions."

"I'd like to talk to your captain before I become involved."

"Sure, he said to tell you to give him a call." He handed her a card. "I gotta get going. I just stopped by to grab a hot dog and meet you. I guess I'll see you tomorrow." He stood up and shook her hand. Stewart arrived balancing plates of food. He offered one to Gerry who thanked him and after looking at the strange conglomeration of vegetables quickly excused himself. "Sorry, looks delicious but I gotta get back to the station."

Stewart sat down and Kara took one of the plates. He put the other on the blanket. "Hey, Connor. I made this just for you. Dig in."

The three-year-old stared at the plate for a few moments. "It's all blue!" he said looking up at the two adults.

"Yes, it is. I call it my Blue-Plate End of Summer Special," Stewart proudly declared in his high-pitched Julia Childlike voice.

Connor cautiously moved the plate away from Celia and whispered in her ear. "You can come live with us if you want."

Celia hiccuped.

☙

9

What was any art but an effort to make a sheath,
a mold in which to imprison for a moment
the shining elusive element which is life itself-
life hurrying past us and running away,
too strong to stop, too sweet to lose.

-Willa Cather, *The Song of the Lark*

THE TRAFFIC ON TOWER Hill Road heading south toward the
beaches was at a standstill. Selina was thankful she was traveling in
the opposite direction toward the Shady Lea Historic District where she'd
recently rented a studio in the 1870 Gothic/Federal style red brick complex which housed a varied group of artists. She looked in the rear-view
mirror to see if she was being followed, then turned right on to Shady Lea
Road past housing built in the 19th century for the Springdale Factory
workers. The sturdy fabrics manufactured at the mill were first sold to
plantation owners for use as clothing for field workers, later for miners
during the Western Gold Rush period, and then for the Union Army's
woolen blankets.

Ambrose Reisert operated a metal staple business from 1955 until
the 1980's and it was Reisert who gave space for a woodworker to carve
his artwork which led to later dividing up the mill into studios for local
artisans and craftspersons. Only a few cars were parked outside along the
water's edge. She looked for the Harley before driving her car around to the
back of the building where it would not readily be seen. From the trunk
of the car she gathered a large bag of sand and hauled it up to the second

floor dropping it outside a set of double doors. She returned to the car to retrieve two bags containing supplies and a few groceries. The owner, Lynn Krim, Ambrose's daughter, met her at the door.

"Hello, Selina. I'm happy to see you've settled in. Do you need help with those bags?"

"No, but thanks. It's quiet here today."

"End of summer. But things should be gearing up later in the fall when everyone will be getting ready for the open studios event in December. Will you be participating?"

"Perhaps. Most of my art is commissioned or in museums. I'm working on something at the moment, but it's for myself. I don't intend to sell it."

"I'll have to come by next time you're here to see it."

"And you can tell me some more stories about the spirits that haunt the building. I often see figures roaming the corridors. There's one who scares me a bit. An old guy with a scar. He never speaks to me."

"He never speaks to anyone. He's been part of the mill from the first day I began opening studios for artists. He spends most of his evenings here and is on friendly terms with the other spirits who inhabit the nooks and crannies of this place. I think they're the only ones he communicates with."

"I'd love to learn more about the history of this building and its inhabitants. Especially the ghosts."

"It's a date. Take care and don't forget, if you're planning on staying late, bring your car around to the other side so you don't end up locked in and unable to leave. You'd have to stay for the night and then maybe you'd get to meet some of our spirits, yourself."

"I actually think I might like that," she called back to her friend as she closed the door of the mill and then turned to go up the narrow staircase.

The studio was in the middle of a long hallway. She listened to see if she could detect the sounds of other artists working, but there was only silence from behind the nearby doors. She carried the cloth bags into a large rectangular room with high ceilings and open beams which she had divided with screens into a working space when you first came in the doors and a sitting area at the far end. The two dividers spanned the width of the room with an opening in the middle. Selina had painted beach scenes on canvas, adhering them to the wooden frameworks behind which was a cozy little nook with two overstuffed chairs and hassocks covered in a floral chintz fabric and a deep blue brocaded camelback sofa. Beach prints, textiles, and photographs of varied sizes hung on the walls behind the sitting area.

The room held a lingering chill from the night before and she switched on the infrared quartz heater housed in the Duraflame wall mantel she had positioned along the right wall space. Sitting atop the mantel was a large carved glass wave of deep aqua melding into a lighter sea of green. All of the art she'd surrounded herself with in this sitting area reminded her of the ocean and was created by the various artists who shared the mill space.

Her own creations were displayed on the floors and the shelves lining the work area which took up most of the room. Although she had been commissioned to create outdoor sculptures in the beginning of her career, she had been spending much of these later years using different materials to fashion smaller, more delicate works. But at the moment, she was involved in finishing a large piece which now took up most of the floor.

A child's sandbox made of dark teak with a seat in each of the four corners held a white alabaster castle which rose up from the center, its turrets pointing toward the ceiling. The structure itself was complete but tiny carvings, some unfinished, were strewn about on a blue tarp. Selina cut open the bag of sand with a point chisel and poured the contents into the box. She took off her sandals and stepped inside to smooth out the mixture around the castle and then sat wiggling her toes in the coolness of the sand. She leaned over to take some shells she had formed from clay and placed them in a pile by her feet. Putting a hand into her jacket pocket, she brought out pieces of sea glass and tossed them into the air to fall as they may around the base of the castle. Closing her eyes, she listened to the sound of the Mattatuxet River flowing through the woods outside the windows of her little sanctuary, her safe place where no one would be able to find her. No one would be able to reach her. No one would be able to hurt her. She thought she heard a slight tapping. She froze for a moment.

"Lynn, is that you?"

No answer. She stepped out of the sandbox and moved tentatively across the wood plank floors toward the doors, putting her ear against a thick panel. "Lynn?" No further sound came from the corridor.

"Perhaps it's only a ghost," she whispered, touching the secured bolt and checking the door handle to make sure it was locked before she grabbed a three-toothed chisel and went behind the safety of the screens. She clenched the tool, holding it straight out in front of her, listening for any sound to tell her he was out there waiting. There was only silence.

ßß

10

*For one's children so often gave one's own
perceptions a little thrust forward.*

-Virginia Woolf, *To the Lighthouse*

RUTH BOUGHT STEWART A set of W. C. Fields' movies for his birthday and lately he couldn't resist quoting lines from the films, mimicking Fields by talking out of the side of his mouth with his lips closed. This morning he entertained his family while making breakfast. "I cook with wine, sometimes I even add it to the food." Kara tried to look amused without encouraging him too much. He sometimes got carried away with his imitations.

Stewart turned his attention to Celia, pointing the spatula at her. "Never cry over spilled milk. It could be poisoned." She was more appreciative than her mother and gleefully waved her little fists. "Ah yes, my little chickadee. Start every day off with a smile and get it out of the way." He flipped a pancake on the griddle.

"Those smell delicious."

"We aim to please, my deeaahh!"

She thought this could definitely be up there with the most annoying impressions he'd ever done. "I'm going to make a special note to thank Ruth for giving you all of those old movies for your birthday," she muttered.

"Tell her I've watched them enough to memorize the best lines." He brought a plate of flapjacks to the table and sat down. "The laziest man I ever met put popcorn in his pancakes so they would turn over by themselves." Kara closed her eyes tightly and then opened them wide. For an incredulous minute, she thought her husband was actually beginning to sound exactly like Fields. To her relief, he hadn't suddenly grown a bulbous red nose.

"Well, I'm glad you used the blueberries we picked," she said pouring maple syrup over the perfectly round, golden discs and hoping Fields never had a quote about fruit.

"I've got a fun night planned. I'll make us a surprise snack. We can have a W. C. Fields' marathon and binge watch all of the movies together."

He said this in his normal voice and Kara hoped he'd run out of material. "Sounds wonderful." She quickly took the opportunity to change the subject. "And what are you up to today?"

"I have a department meeting at the college and then I need to check and see if the bookstore has all of the materials in for this semester's classes. Are you still planning on going to the forensics lab?"

"I am. Sophia's volunteered to babysit Celia. She'll be here around eleven. I'm going to spend some time with Professor Hill. He's examining the evidence from the hit and run and asked if I'd help. He called yesterday to talk. I haven't seen him in a month, and I think he misses me."

"It's good you're getting back into it again. The case sounds like it might be interesting. My meeting's not until one, so I can take care of Celia until Sophia gets here."

They began clearing up the breakfast dishes and he brought the baby into his study to keep him company while he worked.

Celia stared up at the ceiling from her playpen, her tiny hands and feet waggling. Every so often he would look over and say something to reassure her he was still in the room. She gurgled and he put his pen down on the table. "Are you having fun, my little chickadee?"

She answered in a tiny voice, "Dahdah".

He couldn't believe it. The baby was starting to talk. Wasn't she too young for actual words? Maybe it was just his imagination? He stood up, waiting to hear her repeat what he thought he'd heard but there was only silence. He bent over the side of the playpen. She smiled. "Dahdah". This time it was a bit louder and clearer.

"Ssshhhhhhhh." Stewart plucked up his daughter and quickly looked into the kitchen to see if Kara had heard. But she was on the phone and not paying attention to what was happening in the next room.

"Dahdahdahdahdah."

He carried the baby back into the study as she murmured a soft chorus of dahdah's. He closed the door and sat on the couch gently bouncing her up and down. "Good girl, Celia. Can you say momma? Say momma, Celia. Mommamommamomma."

"Dahdahdahdahdah," she answered.

"Mommamommamomma." He waited expectantly.

She found the new game they were playing amusing and he thought he heard a soft chuckle followed by "Dadada!"

This was an emergency. Her first word should be momma. Stewart looked for his cell phone to call Sophia but just then Kara opened the door. "What are you two up to? Are you helping Dad with his homework? Come on. It's time for your morning nap." She took Celia into her arms and kissed the dark curls covering her forehead.

"Googoogaga."

"Googoogaga indeed. What a smart baby. That was Auntie Sophia on the phone. She's going to babysit for you today while mom and dad are working. Say 'Bye, bye, Daddy'."

Stewart held his breath.

"Googoogaga."

"It appears our child has a very limited vocabulary. I'm sure Sophia will fix that."

"We can only hope," he answered as his two favorite girls left the room.

After Kara drove down the driveway, Stewart waited expectantly with the baby in his arms. When Sophia arrived, he met her on the porch. "I need your help. You have to teach Celia to say momma before Kara gets home tonight." He handed her the baby.

"Hello, Sweetie Pie. Is your daddy a little bit nuttier than usual today? Tell him it's much too early for you to have a vocabulary lesson. We won't be starting to work on our words for a few months."

"But she is saying words. She's been saying dada all morning and it's important to me that the first word Kara hears from her is momma."

"Are you sure she isn't just making sounds?"

"She looks straight at me and says dada. I've tried to get her to stop, but it only makes it worse."

They both waited for a sound, but the baby just smiled at them and drooled.

Stewart shook his head. "Okay, then. I'll just be heading out. You two have fun." He gave them a feeble wave as he left.

After he'd gone, Sophia brought Celia up to the nursery. "Let's get you ready to go on an adventure with your auntie. I made you a spiffy outfit especially for our field trip." Sophia reached into her bag and brought out a cotton dress with colorful fish in the design and a hat to match. "Since your daddy is a scientist, I thought we'd go to the Biome Center to see lots of pretty sea creatures."

Celia smiled.

"I knew you would be pleased. Now let me hear you say, 'Auntie'.

"Aga."

"Close enough. We can work on that in the car."

Cʒ

Professor Hill was looking at the evidence collected the night of the hit and run. Morgan's clothes were laid out on the table and he was examining the soles of a pair of running shoes. Kara donned a cover-up, shower cap, and a pair of gloves before she started to work.

"I wish we could afford one of those new trace machines that vacuums up the evidence. I priced them at about forty thousand bucks. It would make it a lot easier for us. He handed her a file. "I've looked over the victim's clothes and recorded my findings, but I'd appreciate you giving them a second glance and telling me what you see."

The blood had dried, forming a rust-colored crust on the material. Tire tracks were visible on the back of the pants and top. Minute glass particles were imbedded in the tread pattern. Kara studied the tracks. "So, this is how they determined it was her car?"

"When the police went to her house, the car was in the garage. The right front head light was cracked and there was blood on the ground underneath the chassis. We examined the blood samples and confirmed it was hers. Except for the headlight, the car didn't sustain any other damage. We took impressions from the soil at the scene. They matched the tread on her clothes to the tires on the *Alfa Rameo* in the garage."

"I see some traces of glass particles in the weave of the fabric."

"They're from the broken shards found at the scene. No doubt it was her own car that hit her. The way I see it, she was out for a run and before she made the turn on Gibson Avenue to go home, she was struck from behind. But speed wasn't a factor. There would have been more damage if she'd been hit at a higher velocity. It appears the car pinned her legs and stopped before it ran over her torso. No skid marks anywhere along the road. Here's the medical examiner's report."

Kara sat reading the report, intermittently asking Hill questions. When she finished, she thought for a while. "Did the team get any prints, fibers, hair or other trace evidence from the outside of the car or the driver's seat?"

"A partial palm print was found on the back of the rear-view mirror. Probably when it was being re-adjusted. Not enough to get a match in the system. But it appears the killer may have donned gloves at some point because the only other prints were Morgan's."

"No blood was inside the vehicle?" Kara asked.

"No blood, skin, or hair on the leather seats or padded steering wheel. Minute traces of glass and cork on the accelerator pedal. But receipts in the glove compartment indicated the car was regularly detailed at a local shop. It had last been done a week ago. It was pretty clean. Fingerprints on the door handle were the victim's but they were smudged which could mean they were smudged by someone wearing gloves."

"Lack of trace could imply the killer wore some kind of protective clothing."

"It was raining that night so, maybe a raincoat with a hood?"

"What about footprints?"

"None at the scene. The street was tarred, and nothing was found in the grass on the roadside. The garage floor was mostly dirt and crushed stone. Old oil build-up mixed with blood around the chassis. Nothing there. But the team was able to get a cast of a fresh tire tread which didn't fit the victim's car in the grassy area along the porch in front of the house."

"It doesn't appear there's much to go on. This was definitely planned in advance. The murder was premeditated."

"It wasn't an accident," Hill concurred. "The tire print and evidence collected from the floor on the passenger and the driver's side of the car is in the other room when you're ready to go through it with me."

They carefully put the clothing back into bags and moved on into the room across the hall where two labeled boxes were on a long counter. Kara donned another pair of gloves before examining the contents of the container marked, FLOOR ON DRIVER'S SIDE. She separated the bits of gravel and soil and stopped. "You're right, this looks like cork to me." She pointed to a minute tan fleck.

"But there was no sign of anything made of cork on the victim, at the crime scene or in the garage. We're not sure of its origin."

"And these glass slivers, do they match the broken headlight?"

"Yes. There was glass on and around the body. We think the killer got out of the car, stood near the victim, and then brought the glass back into the car before leaving the scene. We can look over the car, if you like. "

"That's sounds like a plan and then I'd like to examine the crime scene and the garage."

She examined the broken headlight and checked under the car. "There isn't much damage, except to the headlight."

Kara opened the door and looked around the interior. "The autopsy listed her height at 6'2. She's taller than me. This seat seems to be pushed forward." She lowered herself into the vehicle and placed her left foot on the brake pedal. "Do you think the police may have moved it?" She noted the placement of the rear-view and side mirrors.

Hill opened the folder he was holding. "The report notes that the seats had not been moved although they did open the glove compartment on the passenger side and took out the owner's manual and other papers. I have them here. The car was registered to a Lenore Duckworth."

"That would be her mother. You say only the palm print was found on the back of the mirror?" She was well aware this would be the best place to find a print if the mirror had been adjusted.

"Just the one," he answered.

"We should take another measurement of the seat from the brake pedal." Kara took out her phone and began taking photos. "And I'd like to drive to the Duckworth house and then to Gibson Street where she was killed."

She scanned the papers and the photos from the crime scene contained in the file while the professor drove to the Duckworth estate. They parked in the driveway. She got out to study the area in front of the stairs where the tire print had been taken. She could smell the salt air and hear the sound of the ocean coming from the back of the house. This was a much different area than the one she'd grown up in although it was only a few miles from her old neighborhood in Wakefield.

The Duckworth property wreaked of old money. Back in the early 1900's, during the humid summer months, the Narragansett Pier Rail-road connected to Kingston Station and brought tourists to hotels lining the beaches along the shores. The structures that were later built above the cliffs on Ocean Road foreshadowed the decline of those grand hotels frequented by wealthy families who vacationed away from the larger city mansions where they lived during the rest of the year. Unlike those titans of industry, the Vanderbilts and Astors, who summered across the Bay in Newport, in Narragansett, bankers, doctors, and other entrepreneurs commissioned well-known architects to build these summer getaways for their families to enjoy and to entertain their friends. Robert Dun's *Dunmere*; Samuel Colgate's *Sea Breeze*; Isaac Emerson's *White Hall*. Kara fondly remembered Sunday afternoon drives when her father took the family past the tall gates and stone walls and she and her sister and brother would crane their necks to see if they could catch sight of the rich people who lived in such grand houses.

Kara followed Professor Hill and waited for him to open the doors to let the late afternoon light into the empty garage. A barn sparrow flew down from the rafters and out into the rhododendron bushes near the port cochere. A white residue remained on the places where the police had brushed for prints. She stood looking in and then turned and cast a sweeping glance on the surrounding area. She noted an indent in the laurel hedge, and walked over to look down a short, narrow path leading to the property next door.

"Seen enough?" Hill call out.

She turned and nodded.

He closed the garage doors. "Are you ready to leave?"

"On to the witches' altar. This will bring back memories of when my friends and I used to go there on Halloween."

"And why would you do that?" Hill asked.

"It's a graveyard, Dennis. A graveyard on Halloween! It was crazy scary and part of local folklore."

"What folklore?"

"Don't you know about Joseph Hazard and his fascination with the occult?"

"Of course. I know something about the Hazard Family. They were mill owners – textile mills in Peace Dale in the early 1900s."

"Joseph was born in 1807 - one of the sons of Rowland and Mary Peace Hazard – a bit of a character. His parents were dedicated to helping the community. He found other interests to dedicate himself to partly because he wasn't really interested in the family business. But they were well-to-do, so as an adult, he traveled to England, visited Stonehenge, and came back to RI believing that the spirit world was anxious to communicate with him. He kept journals and the later ones had daily reports on his pocket watch, which he believed was a medium for spirit communications. He was both clairvoyant and clairaudient. And there are letters where he recorded some of his experiences. Like when he believed he scored eleven points in a billiards game through divine intervention. You can read them if you'd like. They're in the special collections department in the Adams Library at Rhode Island College."

"As fascinating as that all sounds, it would entail going north on Rte. 95. You know I avoid going past the Tower on Route 1 and leaving South County whenever possible."

She laughed. "There are three trunks of his memorabilia at the Peace Dale Library if you want to stay closer to home."

"And how do you know so much about this guy?"

"I did a paper on him in my freshman year in college. It was a time when I was reading a lot about the occult. Ruth was my professor for the course. She could see, in addition to all of the information on Joseph's paranormal experiences, I did a ton of research on local history. She gave me an A+ and asked if she could keep it."

"So, he spoke to an invisible friend living inside his timepiece. Sounds like a weirdo to me."

"He preferred to call himself a spiritualist. If you take the next turn, I can show you his castle."

"He built a castle?"

"He loved architecture. It's just around the corner from here. He called the property *Seaside Farm*. It's a private school now."

"How did I not know this was here?" Hill marveled at the Gothic stone structure.

"You need to get out of that lab more. The tower's height was determined so that the séance room on the third floor was closer to the spirits. It did have a practical use. During WWI the castle housed nannies and children from London and was a workstation for code breakers. Now to the scene of the crime. I want to check the mileage. Morgan ran a five-mile circuit most nights. There's a pathway leading to *Druidsdream* from here but it's a walking path. I'm pretty sure she must have come home by way of Hazard Avenue past Earles' Court Water Tower."

"What's this *Druidsdream*?"

"It was used as a guesthouse. It's set back a ways from the road where the accident took place and is adjacent to the graveyard."

"Is Joseph buried there?"

"He'd planned to be entombed where the witches' altar is ringed by eight stone columns. But the family buried him in Portsmouth."

They parked by the side of the road. A fragment of yellow tape was lying against the fieldstone wall leading to the historic graveyard and to the foundation where a monument once rested. "This is the Witches' Altar. And that house over there is *Druidsdream*."

"Is anyone living in it?"

"It's privately owned but this piece of property is public." She walked with him toward the house and stopped next to a stone structure. "This is the Druid's Seat."

"It looks more like the Druid's Uncomfortable Lounge Chair." He sat down and scanned the surrounding wooded area. Kara sat next to him. "Did this thing just drop from the sky?"

"No, Joseph found it on the beach and had it hauled here. Those stone columns are etched with memorials to his mother and family. You can still make out some of the words."

He walked around them reading the names and dates carved into the stone. "And this is where you and your friends spent your Halloweens?"

"Not all night. We did go to Brickley's for ice cream before we went home."

"Now that's a tradition I like."

"Then lead on. I'm feeling the urge for a hot fudge sundae. My treat."

"Guess I'll be having a double banana split for dinner."

Kara cast a final glance at the accident scene and stooped to gather up the remnants of the yellow caution tape on her way to the car.

ᗄ

11

No mother is ever, completely,
a child's idea of what a mother should be,
and I suppose it works the other way around as well.

-Margaret Atwood, *The Handmaid's Tale*

STEWART GAVE HIS WIFE and daughter each a kiss before he left for his early morning class. The phone rang as Kara was cleaning up the breakfast dishes.

"Hi, Kara. It's Gerry Sullivan. The captain said you'd spoken to him and you'll be consulting on this case. I'm going to visit with Mrs. Duckworth. She'll be available later this morning, if you're free."

"I'm not sure I can get a babysitter at such short notice."

"I don't see a problem with you bringing Celia with you, if you don't. What if we meet outside the condo? Number 4 Scenic Vista Drive at about 11:30?"

"We'll be there." She hung up and brought the baby into the nursery. "So, what should you wear to your first interrogation, little one? If Aunt Sophia had some lead time, I'm sure she would have found you a tiny deerstalker hat and a baby trench coat."

Her destination was only twenty minutes away. A discrete sign at the end of a drive informed her she'd reached Sea View Estates. She stopped in front of a speaker. "Kara Langley here to see Mrs. Reginald Duckworth." In less than a minute, the gate automatically opened, allowing her entrance on to the property. She passed the main building and followed the road to the farthest point nearest the water. Number 4 Scenic Vista Drive was tucked in at the very rear of the cul de sac. Gerry was waiting out front by the side of his car.

"Hey, thanks for agreeing to do this. Mrs. Duckworth was supposed to be here. I confirmed last evening when we spoke, but I rang the bell and there was no answer. The door leading to the garage is unlocked and there's a 1974 *Cadillac Deville* in mint condition inside. Maybe she's up at the clubhouse? It's almost lunch time."

"Okay, you go ahead. I'll be right there." She checked on Celia who was sleeping in her baby seat then went inside the garage. She stooped down to check the car's tires and found the tread to be relatively free of any vestige of dirt. Opening the driver's side door, she sat in the seat noting the relatively low mileage on the odometer. She went around to the passenger side to gain access to the glove compartment. She scanned the car's registration which she found under the owner's manual before placing it back.

Celia was waking up. "It's such a nice day. Would you like to take a walk with your Mom?" The baby waved her arms when she saw Kara strap on the snuggy baby carrier. A curtain shifted slightly in an upstairs' window and Kara gave a slight nod to whoever was watching before she and Celia set off down the driveway.

The clubhouse was bustling with older, well-dressed people standing around with drinks, chatting and filling their plates with hors d'ouevres from a buffet. Other residents could be seen settling at their tables in the spacious dining room. Kara joined Gerry in the foyer. He was speaking with a woman seated in a maroon leather barrister's chair behind a highly polished mahogany desk. An aquarium covered the entire expanse of the wall behind her. Kara turned to the side and Celia peeked out from the wrap, mesmerized by the colorful fish moving back and forth, up and down.

"Ms. Nailor, this is Detective Langley …."

"Well, hello, Kara." She stood. "I've known Ms. Langley long before she became a detective," she explained moving from behind the desk. "I was a counselor at the university when Kara was a student." She turned her attention to the baby. "Celia, you are getting to be quite a big girl." Celia gave the woman a glance, but her attention returned to the tiny creatures swimming around in front of her.

"Are you helping with the inquiry into Dr. Duckworth's death?"

"I've been doing some work at the forensics lab and agreed to help, if I can."

"Lenore Duckworth hasn't been here at the clubhouse today. She often takes her meals at her place, although, sometimes she has dinner in the evening with some of the women from the bridge club. I called her number and there was no answer. According to the ledger, she hasn't requested limo service. I expect the *Cadillac* is still in the garage."

"Yes, the door was unlocked," Gerry answered. "Could she have gone out with someone?"

"That's entirely possible. Our residents are free to come and go as they please and she does have visitors who take her out to a restaurant, or the theater, or to shop. She keeps herself busy."

"Thank you, Ms. Nailor." Gerry turned to leave. "Sorry for the inconvenience, Kara. I'm going back to the station. If Mrs. Duckworth returns, maybe you could speak with her? Anything you can find out will be a help."

"I'll wait around for a while, Gerry. I haven't seen my friend, Pat in a long time." He left them as a dapper man sporting a bright red and yellow polka-dotted bow tie approached from a set of double doors to the right of the dining room.

"I appreciate your covering for me, Patricia. You'll be glad to know the brake on Mr. Durfey's wheelchair has been fixed and he will no longer be doing his version of bumper cars in the library.

"Kara, this is Mr. Statler. He is in charge of keeping everyone safe around here. Mr. Statler, this is my friend, Kara Langley and her daughter, Celia."

"Nice to meet both of you. The young lady appears to be quite taken with our aquarium."

"I'm not sure she'll ever want to leave, Mr. Statler."

"Well if you two would like to catch a bite to eat, I'll hold her for you and introduce her to all of the inhabitants of our indoor pond."

"My grandson, Henry helped Mr. Statler give them all names. He's wonderful with children. You could join me for lunch and spend a little time to do some catching up."

Kara took a bottle out of her bag and placed it on the desk. "In case she gets fussy." Pat helped take Celia from the snuggy and transferred her into Statler's arms. The baby's eyes left the fish for a few moments to admire the colorful bow tie. He pointed to a chubby, golden fish. "Now that one there is Mrs. Pauls and the handsome tetra following close behind is her beau, Mr. Van der Camp."

The women chuckled and left the two new friends to their play date. They sat at a table for two near the entrance of the dining room where Kara could keep an eye on her daughter in case she was needed.

"This is a pleasant surprise, Pat. Are you working here now?"

"I work at the college two or three times a week. I'm semi-retired although I have agreed to do some counseling here at Sea View. I have an office just around the corner of this building on this floor where residents are welcome to come and spend time. My door is always open. Our conversations are more social than business, although I do take referrals from family members, if they have a particular concern about a loved one living here."

"I can imagine that would be a comfort when something unforeseen happens."

"I've found it is."

A young waiter came to their table and they both ordered from selections written in navy blue calligraphy in a small ivory booklet edged with a gold leaf pattern.

"Obviously, the people who live here can well afford private therapists but the administration feels it's sometimes a comfort to talk with someone familiar who has a counseling background and can provide an empathetic ear."

"You said the residents come and go as they please." Kara looked around the room.

"A few appear infirmed. If it's found they're experiencing signs of dementia, would any safeguards be in place?"

"Yes, as in any facility with an aging population, we take that into account when they buy a property. They have the option to move into an annex next to this building with staff who specialize in patients having memory issues. Of course, their privacy is respected with their safety a priority."

"I have to admit, I didn't know this place existed until Gerry asked me to come with him to speak with Mrs. Duckworth."

"It's very exclusive and advertises only by word of mouth, as you can imagine. Lenore Duckworth bought her townhouse when this development was in the design stages, although she didn't move here full time until later."

"Yesterday, I visited the Duckworth estate on Ocean Road. It's an impressive old structure. I understand she has living quarters on the top floor. Maybe that's where she is today?" Kara asked.

"Lenore doesn't go there often. She's told me how comfortable and safe she feels here. When she first arrived, she seemed afraid to leave."

"Was she agoraphobic?" Kara was curious.

"I wasn't exactly sure so I asked if she would like to go out to lunch with me and she was hesitant. I gradually convinced her to go into Wakefield on Ladies' Night and we enjoyed a pleasant evening. She loves to window shop. I suggested we take a drive to Providence to go to the museum, but she prefers roaming around the smaller villages. She loves Wickford. A friend of the Duckworth family has a workspace at the artist village nearby. Have you ever been to the Mill at Shady Lea in North Kingstown? It's amazing. Individual studios housed in a large rabbit warren of corridors. Glass blowers, painters, textile art, pottery, sculptors …"

Kara interrupted her. "Sculptors? Did you happen to meet her friend?"

"Oh, yes. Selina Borelli. She's done many pieces for some of the wealthier families in the area and there's even one in front of the sea wall at the Pier."

"I recognize the name."

"She was close with Morgan throughout college. Lenore adores Selina. She regards her as family. I imagine that's why you're here today. To speak with Lenore about her daughter's death. The police didn't have much luck when they came the first time. Just after they discovered Morgan had been struck and killed."

"Yes, Gerry described Mrs. Duckworth as being somewhat distracted. He thought it might be easier for her to provide him information if another woman was present."

"That was very perceptive. And of course, your decision to bring Celia would make it even less threatening. Much kinder. It's a difficult time for any parent when they lose a child, but these circumstances are especially heartbreaking."

Their food arrived and they commented on the lovely presentation.

"I never want to undo the intricate embellishments our chef does with herbs and flowers. She takes pride in her work. Every plate is a piece of art." Pat picked up a small orchid flower and a radish shaped like a rose, placing them by the side of her plate.

"My friends created an herb garden for me when Celia was born. I'm sure she'll love the smell of this parsley and rosemary." Kara tucked the sprigs into a pocket. "Did you ever meet Morgan?"

"We bumped into her in one of the stores while shopping in Wickford. Lenore was at the register purchasing a silk scarf and Morgan came up to her and tapped her on the shoulder. There was no hug or kiss on the cheek. Just the tap on the shoulder. Lenore introduced me, explaining who I was. It was somewhat awkward at the time. While her mother was waiting for the scarf to be gift wrapped, Morgan pulled me aside and asked who she would speak to about transferring her mother to the Alzheimer's unit."

"What a strange thing to say to someone you'd just been introduced to."

"I agree."

"How did you handle it?"

"I explained that we didn't have an Alzheimer's unit, per say, and assured her Lenore was doing relatively well on her own. She informed me she was a doctor and was better at determining her own mother's mental state than a mere social worker and then walked off in a huff."

"Did her mother overhear any of your conversation?"

"If she did, it wasn't mentioned. She didn't even seem to think it was odd that Morgan had left without saying good-bye to her."

"And you haven't seen nor spoken to her daughter since then?"

"She hasn't been to visit in over two years, according to Lenore. But I know Lenore has returned to Ocean Road on a few occasions. A few years ago, she brought me back a lovely china tea set, which she said her mother had given to her for her engagement. I keep it in my office and we sometimes bring it out to the patio to use for special occasions. It always brings back the past and she loves to recount happy times when she was first married. I think that's why she's kept that old *Cadillac*. I'm sure it's worth quite a bit now."

The waiter came to clear away the dishes and asked if they'd like to order dessert.

"I'll have my usual, Corey - a cup of chamomile tea and some strawberries with crème fraiche, please."

Kara looked at Mr. Statler who was resting comfortably with a sleeping baby nestled in his arms.

"I'll pass on dessert, Pat, although it is tempting. You stay and enjoy. I think it's time for me to gather up my daughter and thank Mr. Statler for giving us this chance to chat."

"Call me if you decide to come again to meet with Lenore."

"I'll make sure I let you know and thanks so much for a lovely lunch. Please give Henry, Lilly, and Finn a hug for me."

Kara strolled around the property before she returned to her car. She'd secured Celia into the baby seat, when she heard a voice calling out.

"Halloooo." A woman waved at her from the front door of the condominium.

"Hallooooo there. Were you looking for me?"

"Are you Mrs. Duckworth?"

"Why, yes, I am. And who might you be?"

"Kara Langley, Ma'am."

"And what is the name of your little one?"

"Celia."

"Would you like to come inside? I've made tea."

Kara unstrapped the baby carrier. She moved toward the woman holding open the front door for her to come in. She caught a strong scent of perfume – gardenias - which couldn't hide the smell of liquor on the older woman's breath.

Once inside, they were escorted into the dining room. In the middle of the table was a highly polished silver tea service and three places were set with floral porcelain dessert plates. An antique oak high chair was positioned at the head of the table usually reserved as a place of honor she couldn't help but think. Celia began to wake up as her mother carefully placed the baby carrier onto the chair next to her. Mrs. Duckworth sat across from Celia and Kara.

"Oh, just place her up on the table where she can see everything. Should I be Mother?" the woman asked.

Kara recognized this as something older women once said when hosting a luncheon or a tea party. "Please do."

The smell of Oolong drifted in the air as Lenore Duckworth sat ramrod straight pouring the golden liquid into the dainty cups. "Please help yourself to some pastries." She passed the silver platter with an assortment of cakes over to her guest. "There are some digestive biscuits if little Celia wants to nibble."

Kara took the half empty baby bottle from her bag. "If she's hungry, this should be fine."

But Celia was not interested in food. There was too much for her to see. Emerald green wallpaper with colorful tropical birds balancing on bamboo limbs lined the walls. A sideboard was filled with silver and crystal heirloom frames sporting photos of smiling faces. In the far corner, a large, dome-topped, bronze birdcage held two white cockatoos bathing in the sunlight streaming through double doors leading to the patio. One of them began to pace back and forth on the perch and it suddenly screeched at the guests, grabbing the baby's attention.

"Be quiet Yowie or I'll have to cover your cage."

Kara wished Sophia could see Celia, her blue eyes darting from one new object to the next, reacting to all of the stimulate surrounding her. She would definitely approve.

"Are you looking for a place here at Sea View? I'm afraid it's an over 55 community, but it would be nice to have children running around the property. It can be quite dull, you know, without children."

"I'm just visiting, Mrs. Duckworth. I had lunch with an old friend. Ms. Nailor."

"I know her - Patricia Nailor. I love to spend time with her. She's a wonderful listener. People nowadays don't seem to want to listen to old fogies like me ramble on about the past. I wish I could go back in time. I wish I could live there again."

"What did you like about the past, Mrs. Duckworth?"

"Oh, please call me Lenore. And what was your name again, dear?"

"Kara, and this is my daughter, Celia"

"What a precious little girl. I have daughters, you know. Morgan and Angela and Selina. We often have tea together and Morgan sits where you are now but her little sister must stay buckled up in the high chair so she won't fall and get hurt. It's important to keep children safe, you know."

"Tell me about your girls, Lenore. How old are they?"

"Morgan is seven and Angela is two. They're not here right now, but I'm sure they'll be back in time for late afternoon tea."

"Where do you think they are?"

"Oh, the baby is with Nanny Green upstairs in the nursery and Morgan is playing somewhere outside. Selina's hiding in the boxwood hedge. Probably clipping the bushes into animal shapes. Sculpting green animals. Would you like more tea?" After she poured another cup for Kara, she began to tell about a trip she had taken with the girls to an estate in Portsmouth called Green Animals Topiary Gardens. "I loved the teddy bear and the ostrich. Such fine detail. Would you like more tea, Dear? Oh, I see you still have almost a full cup. I'll just freshen mine up a bit." She took a Waterford crystal decanter from beside the creamer and poured a dark amber liquid into the cup. Her hand shook as she daintily sipped the contents and then wiped her lips with a starched linen napkin.

"Will you be going out at all today, Lenore?"

"Oh, no. I've somehow misplaced my car keys. But if I wanted to go anywhere, I could call Richard. He's been such a dear." She slipped her hand into a pocket and took out a pill case with a blush pink cameo on the top. "I find these tend to relax me." She daintily slipped a capsule onto the tip of her tongue and brought the teacup to her lips. "I always take a little nap after tea-time. A refresher before Reginald comes home from work."

"That's a very good idea. Celia is just about ready for her nap, too. We must be going home."

"Thank you for spending time with me. I would love to talk with you again."

"That would be nice. I'll leave my card for you. Please give me a call."

After she had safely strapped the baby seat in the back, Kara phoned Pat, explaining the situation. "I don't think she should be driving. The good news is she's misplaced her keys."

"Lenore values her independence, but our residents understand their safety is our priority. Although her car is in the garage, I've been informed by Mr. Statler that the rotor arm under the distributor cap is in another place altogether. I am worried about the pills and the alcohol. Not a good combination. I imagine Morgan's death has had a greater effect on her than I thought. I'll go check on her right now. Thank you for letting me know about the situation, Kara. I'll inform her doctor and we'll keep a close eye on her."

ᘓ

When she'd put a very tired Celia safely in her crib, Kara phoned Gerry Sullivan to tell him about her time with Lenore Duckworth.

"Thanks. You've saved me a trip back this evening to see if I could talk to her. You seem to have gained her confidence. I'd be glad if you followed up with her. Hopefully, you'll catch her when she's in a better frame of mind. Anything you can find out will be of help. I have some other leads to follow up on and I'm waiting for documents from the Duckworth's lawyer. I'll be busy for the rest of the week. The Captain told me he'd spoken to you about consulting on this case with us. I appreciate your help."

Gerry hung up and studied the list of potential suspects the team had compiled in the last week. They all had one thing in common – they'd sued Morgan Duckworth for failing to diagnose conditions leading to costly treatments and operations. Those were the lucky ones. They'd survived. Selina Borelli had already come into the station and he'd underlined her name. Some of the former patients had been eliminated as suspects because they lived out of state and their alibis had checked out. Besides Borelli, there were four others who had strong motive and opportunity. One of the names on the list was the husband of a woman who had died, and he had decided not to take part in the group malpractice suit. He'd been into the station and spoken with an officer. Gerry looked over the man's statement. Underlined and in bold letters were the words NO ALIBI Extremely closed-mouth. Seems to have something to hide. Gerry picked up the phone and dialed.

"Mr. Carnavale. This is Detective Sullivan from the Narragansett police. I'd like to speak with you regarding Morgan Duckworth ..... Yes, I know you were in last week. You spoke with Detective Bosquet, but I have a few more questions .... tomorrow morning will be fine. I'll expect you here at the station around ten unless you'd prefer me to go to your place in Kingston?" When Carnavale assured him he'd be at the station the next morning, Gerry hung up and in black marker placed a circle around the suspect's name.

⚗

Selina returned home from her nightly walk on the beach. She put on her pajamas and robe, made herself a cup of cocoa with marshmallow fluff, and sat on the couch with her journal. *Today was quiet at the studio. I seem to have been the only one working except for the weird old man who seems to be lurking around every corner. The way he moves – like Grazio. I followed him once, to get him to turn and look at me, but he's elusive. I tried to see if he worked in one of the studios. He may just be a visitor. I thought I saw him leave the other night on a motorcycle.*

The castle is completed. I'm spending all of my time now on the last maquette. When I was at the worktable today, I felt someone's presence at the window but I looked out into the woods and no one was there. I've had this strangely ominous feeling for the past few days and have taken to locking the door when I work through the night. My imagination has been running wild lately. Spirits and shadows follow me all around the mill. Evie, Grazio, Morgan, my mother - I see their faces everywhere in my dreams and waking hours.

69

Lenore phoned and she wants me to bring her to the old house. She asked why I didn't come in for tea the last time I was there and if I thought the mountain laurel would need pruning before winter. She was slurring her words. I'll have to call her tomorrow because I'm not sure when she wants me to come by. She told me I was her favorite child. It's really strange to think of her as a mother. She's nothing like my own mother. I've been dreaming of her a lot lately. I seem to get more like her every day.

It's getting colder and the old bricks at the mill are holding on to the dampness of the fall nights. I must remember to bring my sweater coat with me tomorrow. The alpaca one Elliot bought for me when we were in Peru. That surely will keep out the cold. He called me from New York. He had a meeting with his agent yesterday and another audition this afternoon. He's promised to come back soon. I feel better when I know he's nearby. I haven't felt safe since my mother died. It seems such a long time ago. I think I'll see if I can find where I put that sweater. I have to pack soon as I'll be closing my house up in another week. Preston has told me he needs me to stay at his place through the fall and into next spring. He doesn't expect to be home until late March. I love having such a beautiful place all to myself. I move from room to room and sleep in a different bed every night. The benefit to not having many belongings is that it makes it easier to move quickly. This summer has been wonderful with the beach right there and Elliot only a few minutes away. It's given me such comfort. I think I hear a car outside. Maybe he's returned earlier than he expected? I know I shouldn't think this way — but I hope he doesn't get the part.

℞

12

THE SMELL OF COFFEE brewing enticed Ruth out of bed before her alarm rang. Usually she was up at least an hour before Rick, but for the past week, her husband rose while it was still dark and was often dressed and working on a project by the time she made it downstairs. This morning he was in the den with one of his large portfolios opened on the desk. She stood behind him and placed her hand on his shoulder looking down at the artwork. As he carefully turned each page, she realized she'd not seen this work before. The dates on the bottom of the pages of sketches and photos went back to a time before they'd met - a time when he'd been married to Yvonne and they'd owned the artists' gallery in Greenwich Village. Some were sketches of New York street scenes during the different seasons, others were photos of storefronts decorated for Christmas.

"Did Gino design these windows?"

"He sure did. I was always so proud to tell people that my brother Gino created the beauty they were admiring."

"And the sketches are Yvonne's?"

"She would go out at all hours to try and capture the feel of the city. Some nights, I would lock up the gallery and go upstairs to find her sitting at the bedroom window with a pile of drawings at her feet. And often she'd set up her easel and try to sketch the faces of some of the people who came through the door to the studio. She called it our little corner of the world."

He turned to the back of the portfolio and on the last page was a photograph he'd taken of a young Yvonne drawing a mother and baby who were standing in front of a pedestal holding a bronze sculpture of a mother and child. "This is my favorite picture of her. She thought she appeared too severe, but that was always the look she wore when she was focusing on something she wanted to capture before it disappeared from sight." He stood up and hid his face in his hands.

"Rick? Is something bothering you? You've been so distant lately."

"I'm just a little tired between my art classes, the special exhibit, and the nights I've been filling in driving the taxi. The late hours are killing me."

"You should tell Bert to hire someone else. You certainly don't need the money now that you're full time at the university. And I would think some of the business is going to Uber drivers, so why does he still need you?"

"College kids aren't very dependable, and he has a tendency to hire the ones who work a few weeks and then disappear. He said he has someone lined up for the late shift, so I won't have to help after next week. You know, I still feel indebted to him for giving me a job when we moved here from New York. It gave me a chance to be with Yvonne during the day, taking her to the doctors and sometimes she even rode along with me at night until she was too sick to leave the house. Bert was good to me when I needed a friend."

She watched as he closed the portfolio and put it back into the closet. "Did you make enough coffee for a second cup and some for me?"

"I brewed a whole pot. I saw the stack of papers on your desk and knew you'd be up early working on them." He kissed her and brushed a wisp of blond hair from her forehead. "Ruth ...." He intended to tell her about the phone call from the police but stopped himself. "Do you have any idea where my wool socks are? I think it's about time I put away my sandals."

She sensed there was something he wasn't saying. They didn't keep secrets from each other, and she knew he would tell her what was bothering him in his own good time.

CB

Gerry Sullivan was taking notes on the file in front of him when the call came in from the front desk that Mr. Carnavale had arrived. He kept the folder open and referred to it immediately after Rick had taken a seat in front of the desk.

"Mr. Carnavale, it's come to my attention that you left out some important information the last time we spoke with you."

"I answered all of the questions you asked."

"You did. But I think you may not have informed us at the time about an argument you'd had with Morgan Duckworth a few weeks prior to her death."

"We didn't argue."

"But you've seen her recently."

"She has a shop in Narragansett. I've seen her around from time to time. We don't speak."

"I'm told you had a disagreement. That you went to speak with her at her shop."

"She wasn't there that day. I gave a message to her business partner."

"You conveniently left that out of your statement," Gerry looked straight at him.

"I was asked by Detective Bosquet if I had talked with Morgan recently and I answered that I had not."

"And what was the message you left for her?"

"You've spoken with her partner, so you already know what it was."

"I'd like you to tell me exactly what you said, Mr. Carnavale."

"I told her to inform Morgan she could keep her money. I had no use for it."

"Are you referring to the settlement from the group lawsuit?"

"I was never part of any lawsuit. You can confirm this with the attorneys. I'm sure you already have the names of everyone involved in the case."

"Then explain your message about keeping her money."

"Morgan mailed me a check. I never asked for anything from her."

"Where is that check now?"

"I ripped it up."

"I have copies of her accounts here and I see she sent you two checks for the same amount. One just a few days before she was killed."

"If you have her account information, you'll see neither was cashed."

"Mr. Carnavale, where were you the night Morgan Duckworth was killed?"

"I worked for the South County Cab Company that night. I was filling in for a driver who didn't show up."

"I have the scheduling information for that night, and it appears you were working until 2am." Detective Sullivan handed a set of papers to Rick. "There's a fare you took to the Coast Guard House around 9:15. We confirmed it with the couple. But there's a long period of time after you dropped them off and when you picked up your next fare that's unaccounted for. Where were you, Mr. Carnavale?"

"It wasn't very busy, so I grabbed a coffee and went over to the beach parking lot to take a break."

"Where did you get the coffee?"

"The drive-through at the Dunkin' Donuts."

"Which Dunkin' Donuts, Mr. Carnavale?"

"The one across from Salt Pond Shopping Center."

"Could you describe the person who waited on you?"

"It was a kid."

"Girl or boy?"

"A boy."

"Can you describe him for me? I'll be interviewing anyone who worked there that night and it would help to narrow it down a bit."

"He wore a cap but he had dark hair. Skinny, tall. He wore glasses."

"Is there anything else you can tell me about your shift that night?"

"It was uneventful. A couple going to the Coast Guard House for dinner. A fare from a bar on Boon Street. He was pretty drunk."

"Where did you take him?"

"He asked me to drop him off outside the condos across from the town beach. I didn't see which unit he went into."

"You haven't been much help, Mr. Carnavale. Please understand you're a person of interest in this case and we'll be speaking with you again after we've looked into what you've told us. Don't leave the area without informing us of where we can reach you."

Rick stood up to leave.

"Are you sure you haven't got anything else to tell us which would help you?"

"I assure you, I won't be going anywhere. Call me in when you've gathered your facts, Detective."

Rick left the station and drove to the Fine Arts Building on campus. Students were putting up an exhibit and he spent the rest of the morning helping them. At lunch time, Ruth surprised him in his office.

"Hey, I brought you some lunch from Rhody's at the Emporium. Spinach pie."

"I was going to go out in a while to get something to eat. You saved me a trip. Thanks, Hon. How was your morning?"

"Just a class and an uneventful department meeting. Oh, I may be going to a conference in Boston in October. Maybe we could arrange a mini vacation? We could get tickets to the symphony and visit the Isabella Gardner Museum."

"I'm not sure I'll be able to leave the state any time in the near future."

"What do you mean? Something's wrong, isn't it?"

"I was at the police station this morning."

"Police station? Did you stop in to see Kara? Is she helping out with a case?"

"No, I was at the Narragansett station. A policeman called and asked me some questions about the hit and run case and then he said I should come to the station to speak with them."

"Rick, why were they asking you about that? What could you possibly tell them?"

"Unfortunately, more than I cared to." He related to her what had taken place and told her not to worry, although he knew she would and there was nothing he could do to put her at ease.

When Ruth returned to her office, in Roosevelt Hall, she closed the door and called her friend.

"Kara, I hate to impose on you, but we need to talk as soon as possible. I have a big favor to ask."

℁

The Storm

Then up and spake an old Sailor
Had sailed to the Spanish Main,
"I pray thee, put into yonder port,
For I fear a hurricane."

-Henry Wadsworth Longfellow, *The Wreck of the Hesperus*

13

Some things are best learned in calm, others in storm.

-Willa Cather, *The Song of the Lark*

F IRST, THE SOUND OF wood splitting apart. A cracking, then a
dull thud which shook the house. Kara got out of bed cautiously so
as not to wake Stewart. Saturday was the one morning he liked to sleep
in. She went to the baby's room. Unlike her skittish mother, Celia was
still sound asleep like her father. It wasn't just the wind which was keeping
Kara awake. She'd been wrestling with what she was going to do with the
information Ruth had given her about Rick.

From the front porch, she peered into the darkness before dawn, trying
to catch sight of the tree limb she'd heard breaking, but she had to be
content with the thought it, at least, had not fallen on the roof.

Inside, she placed a bagel in the toaster and took out a tub of whipped
cream cheese. It was blue. She wasn't sure if it was moldy or if Stewart had added coloring. Somewhat like Picasso, he was going through a
gastronomic "Blue Period" which she found almost as unappetizing as his
"Green" phase around the holidays when he was using avocados, peas, and
basil, among other ingredients, to add a festive flare to his experimental
recipes. What could he possibly be using to turn their normal kitchen
ingredients blue? She wasn't going to take a chance. She put the tinted
concoction back into the refrigerator, poured herself a glass of blueberry
juice, and munched on the dry bagel as she pondered whether she would
investigate the newest information on the hit and run with or without

Rick's knowledge. She'd already decided she would not be consulting with Gerry Sullivan until she'd learned more about the facts.

In her heart, she knew Rick was not capable of cold-blooded murder. The first time they'd met, she was questioning him about another murder case. She had found him irritably reticent back then, but later, when they became friends, she realized he was a quiet man who kept things to himself. It hadn't surprised her that he'd kept Ruth in the dark about the incident with Morgan and the money. He would see this as being protective. Another word which appropriately summed up his personality.

She opened her email and found one sent the previous evening from Pat Nailor.

> *Kara, Lenore Duckworth asked if I could send you a note in regard to her daughter's memorial service today. She would like you to attend and there will be a small luncheon at her home on Ocean Road afterwards. I know this is short notice, but she was adamant I send you an invitation. Pat*

An attachment with details was included with the email. Kara sent a reply she would be there at the service and the luncheon. That would be as good a place as any to start her own investigation into what she could find regarding the night Morgan was run over. Hopefully, the weather would cooperate, and she could get a start on what could be the most important case she was officially not really a part of.

છ

Kara arrived early and sat in the middle of the chapel. An organ quietly played, its songs stirring up memories for her as people entered, genuflected, and took their seats. During the eulogy, she glanced around and noticed Rick in the back pew. She nodded but he appeared staunchly focused and not attuned to anything around him. Someone else was sitting in the pew, but nearer to the wall. Kara couldn't tell who it was. Two young women had slipped in beside her at the beginning of the service. Four older women who must have been Lenore's friends shivered together on the opposite side of the chapel. They had donned their Sunday best and were ill prepared for the cleaving dampness now surrounding them. Mr. Statler had escorted them in and sat behind them. Lenore wore her long fur coat, black silk gloves, and an ebony velvet hat with a thick veil drawn over her face. It was a somber group who had come to gather in remembrance of Dr. Morgan Duckworth.

The chapel had been built to keep out the harsher elements, but wafts of cold air hung overhead and damp drafts crawled around the feet of those who sat huddled together on the hard wooden benches. Selina pulled the wool up closer to her nose, hiding most of her face. Only her blue eyes were left uncovered between the violet folds of the cashmere scarf and matching toque. She slowly rose to join the other mourners in a familiar song she remembered. The lyrics took on another meaning for her today than they had in the past.

Abide with me, fast falls the even tide, The darkness deepens, Lord with me abide! When other helpers fail and comforts flee, Help of the helpless, Oh, abide with me!

She found she couldn't continue with the verses. Suddenly her lips were dry. Her throat seemed to have closed up, and tears dropped into the softness of the cloth around her neck. She wanted to run from the chapel, but someone else had entered late and now sat blocking the end of the pew. He was not bundled up as the others were. His coat was open and he wore neither hat nor muffler. He stood staring straight ahead, the hymnal open in his ungloved hands, but he did not utter a word of the song. His lips were pressed too tightly together. She recognized her old friend's husband, Rick, the person who had swum out to see if she needed help. *Help of the helpless.* She moved a bit closer to him as the hymn ended and they sat listening to the words in *Isaiah 25:4-5.*

"For you have been a strong place for those who could not help themselves and for those in need because of much trouble. You have been a safe place from the storm and a shadow from the heat. For the breath of the one who shows no pity is like a storm against the wall ...."

The one who shows no pity. Selina thoughts drifted away only to be brought back to the present as someone began a short eulogy followed by the minister's words echoing against the stone, "You rule the stormy sea. You can calm its angry ways."

Stormy sea ... calm its angry ways. She recalled the past week when Elliot had surprised her as she walked along the beach marveling at the warnings the ocean was sending out. The memory of that day was imbedded in her heart and she relived the scene in her journal like a story she would tell, writing the words as she remembered them.

The breakers were throwing their white-foamed fangs up onto the beach, tossing out gifts of glossy olive-colored kelp and worn-ridged shells and pale-colored sea glass only to selfishly reclaim their offerings, pulling them back into the swirling sea. A storm was slowly developing in the warm waters along the coast, taking its time to decide where it was eventually going to wreak its destruction. The smell of thunder was in the air around them as they walked together, his arm guiding her along.

"When are they expecting the hurricane to reach us?" she asked. "I haven't been keeping up with the news."

"There's a front coming through first. High winds and rain. The hurricane is still in the Atlantic off the coast of the Carolinas, so it should take a few more days to reach us unless it turns and tracks farther out into the ocean."

"When you come back to RI, do you have a place to stay?'

"No. This is a rental. I'll need to be out by tomorrow. I've already packed the rest of my things to return to New York, but I promise I'll be a call away if you need me."

"You're welcome to stay at my cottage. I'm house-sitting for a client, so I won't be there, but I'll leave the door unlocked for you."

"Thanks, I may take you up on that offer, although, with this storm brewing, the police will make sure everyone is evacuated if it becomes a hurricane."

"There are tons of empty rooms where I'll be staying, so if you get stuck, you can always come and keep me company. It's high up on the rocks and has weathered tougher storms than any we get around here today. I'll take you there next time you're in town, if you'd like."

Suddenly, Selina was jolted back to the present, no longer on the beach with Elliot. People around her were standing. Lenore Duckworth, the bereaved mother, walked alone down the center aisle. Selina rose and waited until the music had ended and everyone had left. She knelt and said a silent prayer before following the others outside.

☙

Kara had planned to talk with him but Rick had left before she got the chance. She decided to do some discrete investigating without him. On her way to the Duckworth estate Kara stopped at the Cab Company. A young woman was at the desk when she walked in.

"The owner is out right now." Kara was well aware that Bert always went home to his wife for a home-cooked lunch. "And the afternoon driver hasn't arrived."

Kara made a decision to take advantage of the situation.

"I'm not looking for a ride. I think I may have left a glove in the back seat of one of your cabs last night."

"There's a lost and found box on the counter in the garage." The phone rang, interrupting them. "Go ahead in and see if it's there."

Kara ran in and quickly locked the doors of the cabs then returned to the office area.

"It's not in the box and the doors are all locked. Could you unlock them for me?"

The clerk went into the garage and Kara opened the scheduling book on the desk to the night of the hit and run. She snapped photos of the pages and then speed dialed the phone number for the taxi service.

The phone rang and the clerk ran back to answer it. "They're open now. I couldn't find anything but you can go in and check for yourself, if you want." She picked up the phone. "Hello, South County Cab Company. Lisa speaking. How may I help you? Hello?"

"Thanks." Once inside the garage, she examined the front right tires for each vehicle, snapping a photo of one of them. She came back into the office and waved a green mitten. "Got it. Thanks for your help."

"No problem."

ೞ

Rick parked his car in the lot and got out to walk the beach. It felt to him as though the elements were gathering together to create a powerful storm to show everyone that nature held all of the cards. He hadn't told Ruth everything and it weighed on his mind. They didn't keep secrets from each other. But this was something he'd decided to keep from her. Something he didn't want to touch her. His life with Yvonne was tucked away in the past, or at least he'd thought it was until the check arrived. It had angered him that she thought his wife's life could be valued in terms of money. But money was the only thing that ever mattered to Morgan. And that woman was toxic. He couldn't let this poison infect his new life with Ruth. Ruth deserved better. And in the end, Morgan got what he knew she deserved. But now, she was chasing him from the grave and he had to decide what to do. As he walked back to the parking lot, he'd decided. He would disappear for a while. Lay low until things calmed down a bit. He wasn't sure how much they knew about that night, but he didn't want to wait for them to find out. He began to back up the car just as a police van blocked him from moving. Two officers signaled for him to get out.

"Richard Carnavale?" He nodded yes. "You're under arrest for the murder of Dr. Morgan Duckworth. Anything you ..." He heard the handcuffs click and felt the cold metal against his wrists. It was already too late.

ೞ

When Kara arrived at the Duckworth house on Ocean Road, the two labradoodles were running around on the front lawn. They came to her and stood wagging their tails expectantly.

She rubbed the tops of their heads. "Good puppies. Shouldn't you be inside? It's raining and your lovely fur is getting all wet. Come on." They followed her through the open door into the hall where a woman in a maid's uniform complete with white apron helped her off with her coat and hung it in a closet.

"Everyone is being seated, Miss. Go right in." She pointed to her left. The dogs trotted off in the opposite direction from where the voices were emanating.

Most of the guests were seated. There were boxes of imported chocolates on the dining room table each with a place card. She found her chair and sat down next to an attractive woman. Her name card reads Selina Borelli. It was the woman who was bundled up in the back pew. She counted the seats at the table – thirteen. Lenore was at the head with Pat to her right. Everyone from the service was there except for Rick.

"Hello, I'm Kara Langley." She turned to face the woman.

"Selina Borelli. Have we met before? You look familiar."

"I don't think so, but I recognize your name from your artwork. You have a studio at Shady Lea … I've been there for the open studio exhibits."

Lenore began to speak, thanking all of them for supporting her at this difficult time. She signaled for the shrimp salad to be served and her guests began to eat while conversing quietly with those closest to them. Rick's chair remained empty. Outside, the wind picked up and began to blow a torrent of hard raindrops against the doors and windows leading to the back yard and the ocean beyond. Kara listened in on the conversations around her. Selina was talking to a woman across the table who introduced herself as Morgan's business partner.

"Will you be carrying on with the herbal store?"

"Oh, yes. It's very lucrative. Morgan wasn't much of a hands-on person, so Chloe and I have been running the place since Mrs. Duckworth set it up for her daughter." The young woman by her side nodded in agreement.

"Mrs. Duckworth is the owner?" Kara joined in.

"Yes, she assured us she would continue to finance the shop and not to worry. She's very generous. She's introduced us to many of our wealthier clients."

"Yes, she's a woman with many important connections. We appreciate everything she's done to make us successful," Chloe chimed in from across the table.

Kara was beginning to wonder exactly what Morgan, herself owned. She knew the estate was still in her mother's name and the apartment in New York, the condo at Sea View, the accounts, and both cars. Morgan's practice no longer existed, and her husband hadn't left her anything. It would have been held up in court until a body had been found or he'd been declared dead after a certain amount of time. But he'd lost his fortune before they'd separated, and Kara made a note to find out exactly what had been in his estate and to whom it had been bequeathed. And was there insurance? Although, if it had been ruled a suicide, nothing would have been settled on a grieving widow. Kara decided she would try to remain after the others left. She had some questions and she hoped Mrs. Duckworth stayed sober enough to give her answers.

The weather was proving to be unpredictable. The rain had quieted down although the wind gusts seemed to get worse. Everyone began to leave soon after coffee and pastries had been served. She spoke with Pat who had to get home to babysit for her grandchildren.

"I can wait and give Lenore a ride to Sea View if she decides she won't be staying for the night," Kara offered.

"Lenore told me she intends to be here for the rest of the week, maybe longer, so I don't think it will be a problem. The maids come in when she needs them, and her friends have agreed to drop by and make sure she's all right. And she's assured me she has the number of someone who will pick her up if she needs to go anywhere. I'll just say my goodbyes. Thanks for coming at such short notice."

Kara stood at the French doors looking out across the veranda and an expansive green lawn which reached to the horizon and then seemed to end suddenly. Kara imagined the cliffs below creating a jagged drop into the waves crashing against the rocks. She turned when Lenore came back into the dining room.

"Can I do anything to help?" Kara moved to clear the table.

"No, Dear. The catering staff will be gone soon. And Mary will clean up before she leaves for the day. Would you sit with me awhile? I could use some company right now."

They moved into the drawing room. Its walls were covered with an embossed paper in a calm blush shade and the room was filled with lovely antiques, polished to a lustrous sheen. Deep pink satin drapes with matching box valances outlined the floor-to-ceiling windows. Stiffel lamps, with their cut crystal bases, gave off a golden glow, warming the inside of the room. The dogs stirred on the hearth where a fire was burning. After closing the curtains to ward off the fog and cold threatening from outside, Lenore sat in a Queen Anne chair opposite Kara who'd sunk into the feather-cushioned couch. "Please help yourself to the chocolates." Lenore opened the box on the table. "I have them sent in from France by the crate load. Could I get you an after-dinner drink?"

"No, thank you. The luncheon was more than enough. You must be tired."

"I haven't taken my afternoon nap, but I'm sure I'll sleep well tonight."

"Will someone be coming to stay with you?"

"The maids come in and out when I call them, but truthfully, I'd rather spend some time alone. And Marie and Pierre are here with me." The dogs' ears twitched upon hearing their names. "I find being surrounded by familiar things very comforting." She picked up a small bronze bird from the table next to her chair and cupped it in the palms of her hands. Selina made this for our twenty-fifth anniversary." She was quiet for a few minutes. "Morgan hated this place and everything in it," she blurted out suddenly. "She came back for her father's funeral. Reginald doted on her. She couldn't find the time to visit while he was sick, but she made it in time to bury him. It was a shock for her when she found out he'd left everything to me. The house, the condo, the cars, the stocks, everything. She'd expected more from him." Lenore bowed her head, her chin touching her chest. Kara barely heard her whisper, "Yet, she gave so little …."

For a moment, Kara thought the older woman had nodded off, but she raised her head and held out the palms of her hands in a questioning gesture. "I can't imagine why she didn't return to New York. She loved the apartment in the middle of all the bustle of the city. She'd still be alive if she'd just stayed where she was."

Kara suddenly remembered Silas, the homeless man in Robert Frost's "The Death of the Hired Man" and sadness washed over her. *He has come home to die. You needn't be afraid he'll leave you this time.*

Lenore interrupted her thoughts. "She had no money. At least the kind of money she'd become accustomed to. Morgan knew I would never turn her away. I don't think she ever, for one minute, thought I'd outlive her - that she wouldn't inherit all of this. In her mind was the belief if she just waited it out, I'd be dead, and she'd be rich again." She'd begun softly talking to herself. "Best she didn't know about the new will." She absentmindedly began stroking the tiny metal sculpture, preoccupied with her own thoughts, forgetting she had a guest until Kara moved slightly causing her to look up. She leaned forward and offered Kara the bronze bird. "Bring this home to Celia."

Kara was momentarily taken by the offer of the gift and the fact the woman had remembered her daughter's name. "Oh, I couldn't take this. It was a present. It belongs here in this room with you."

"I would like to send something home for her. Does she like candy?" She pointed to the box of truffles on the coffee table and then shook her head. "Of course, she's much too young for chocolates. Bring it home to your husband. Reginald and I could go through a box of these together every night after dinner."

Kara rose to leave. "Thank you, Lenore. If there is anything I can do, please call me."

"Maybe you could bring Celia here the next time you visit and we could go up to the nursery and she could choose something herself?"

"That's a lovely idea. I'm sure she'd enjoy a visit. I really must be going so you can rest. Is there something I can do for you before I leave?"

"No, but since you kindly offered, there is something I've been dreading and I know it must be done." She shook her head. "I hesitate to impose on you."

"Please, I'd like to help."

"Perhaps when you return, you could help me sort through Morgan's things. I mean, her clothes. I paid a fortune to keep her well dressed and she had an exquisite sense of style. It's a shame for them to go to waste. Such a difficult job. To clean out what is left behind after a death. Do you know of anyone who would know what to do with them?"

"Actually, I have just the person to help you with that. My friend Sophia is an expert when it comes to appreciating the value of clothes. She'll have an idea or two, I'm sure."

"Oh, please bring her with you the next time. And Celia, too."

"Call when you feel up to some company. You stay where you are. I'll see myself out. Here's my cell phone number should you want to talk."

The dogs jumped up and followed her as far as the porch. She petted both of their heads and they ran back inside to the warmth of the fireplace.

Kara drove her car around the drive and started out toward the road. Frost's wise words took on more meaning as she stopped to look in the rearview mirror at the house now enveloped in fog. *Home is the place where, when you have to go there, They have to take you in.*

Kara took out her cell phone to call Stewart to tell him she was on her way home. She found a text message from Ruth.

Kara, the police have arrested Rick. Please, call me as soon as you get this.

ଔ

14

Once more home is a strange place:
by the ocean a big house now,
and the small houses are memories
once live images, vacant
thoughts here, sinking and vanishing.

-Richard Moore, *Depths*

THROUGHOUT THE NEXT WEEK, the weather continued to be unsettling for everyone. Friday morning ushered in the calm before the brink of the next storm. The town had had its practice run and now the real deal was hurtling up the coast looking for a place to wreak havoc. Television shows were being interrupted for regular updates. Villagers were already scoffing up all the bread and milk they could fit into their reusable shopping bags in preparation for the storm being forecast on every local channel.

The banging of hammers could be heard as homeowners in the beach areas boarded up windows with plywood and placed sandbags around doors and foundations. Those in places which could potentially flood were warned to plan to evacuate and shelters were being set up for anyone who might need somewhere to wait out the storm. Most people were familiar with the fall hurricane season routine in Rhode Island. They also understood that the local weather reports tended to make every storm seem like an impending apocalypse.

"It seems different this year, preparing for a storm with an infant in the house," Stewart commented as he and Gino filled the generator with gasoline and tested it out, making sure it would start if needed. "I've got my chain saw ready in case any more tree limbs come down." They had just finished piling up wood from the branches that had fallen during the high winds the past weekend.

"It's good ta be prepared even dough most a da time dese weather guys get it wrong," Gino advised.

"Right now the best-case scenario is that it could turn from a hurricane to a tropical storm before it makes land fall. The worst of it could veer off into the Atlantic."

"From your lips ta God's ears."

Kara pulled into the yard and drove up to the garage. Gino ran to her. "How's Rick? Is he okay?"

"He seems fine. We've arranged for bail. He has a good lawyer. Everything is going slower than usual because of the storm."

"And he's got you. I know you'll get him off," Gino grabbed her hand.

"I'll do everything I can, Gino. I promise."

He took out a handkerchief and wiped his eyes. "I gotta get goin. Sophia's gonna be workin at da hospital later on today after youse come back from pickin up da clothes. I'm gonna see if Ruth's okay. An I got some work ta do at da Courthouse Center. If ya need anything, call me. I got my cell phone charged up."

They waved as Gino sped off on his motor-scooter. Stewart helped Kara bring groceries into the house. In the kitchen Kara began taking out a supply of paper plates and cups from her shopping bag. "All set outside?" she asked.

"Generator's ready and anything that could fly around is safely stored away. I'm just going to fill the bathtubs with water. When you get home, we'll hunker down and see what happens." He took Celia from her bouncy seat and lifted her high into the air.

"It feels funny. Usually I'm working when there's any threat of a storm. I wonder how everything is at the Safety Complex?"

"They can get through one hurricane without you and we need you with us. Tell your momma how happy you are we'll all be together and safe." The baby laughed as Kara came over to tickle under her chin.

The phone rang. It was Sophia. "Change of plans. I'll meet you at the Duckworth place. We'll take separate cars because I volunteered to do a shift at the hospital this afternoon."

"Sophia, don't bring up Rick's arrest. I want to get as much information as possible while we're there. And if she asks, you can let Lenore know you'd met Morgan but, whatever you do, don't refer to her daughter as 'The Quack'."

"I would never speak ill of the dead. It's really bad karma, Kara. I won't say anything about Morgan unless her mother brings it up. Oh, one more thing - get out the Baby Langley loose-leaf binder. There's a section entitled *Weather*. You can start taking some notes for me on Celia's First Hurricane. See you in an hour."

C3

They'd purposely left their cell phones in the car, cutting off the rest of the world and enjoying the time they had together. Elliot and Selina sat on the beach, bookends frozen in time and place like the sculptures she created for other people. Old friends keeping watch on the waves, whitecaps jumping out of the ocean and lapping at their feet.

"Thanks for offering to let me use your place while I'm here in RI."

"It's yours to use when you need it. I was surprised you returned so soon."

"I didn't have any call-backs today. Everything will probably go on hold in New York due to the storm." He grabbed her hand and pulled her up. "Let's take a walk. I hear one of the last Browning beach cottages is for sale."

"I know there used to be lots of summer houses that have since been destroyed by storms. The 1938 Hurricane devastated the homes and businesses here in Matunuck. But what are the Browning cottages?"

"From what I was told by the real estate person who rented my place to me, around the turn of the century, some preeminent RI families built a cluster of homes on property owned by a local farmer, Browning. They set up a little summer colony and brought their kids here to vacation. Of course, as you're well aware, our definition of cottages today is not quite the same as what the more affluent considered to be cottages in those days."

"How well I know. Their humble abodes would have been magnificent mansions and castles to us commoners."

They strolled along the edge of the water listening to the sound of the waves at their feet and the screeching of the seagulls. Selina stopped every now and then to fill the pockets of her blue sweater with sea glass and shells as they talked about things they'd like to do some day. Elliott pointed to a Victorian clapboard, which obviously had seen better days. "That can be our new home away from home. Come on, let's see what a cool million and a half bucks can get us."

Selina stood frozen, staring at the house on the ridge above them.

"Selina, where's your sense of adventure? Don't you want to explore?"

She shook her head. "Elliot, let's go back."

"Sure, no problem." They walked back in silence to where they'd left their blanket and she sat staring out to sea.

"What's wrong, Selina? We were having such a nice day. Did I say something to upset you?"

"No, it has nothing to do with you. It was me. I suddenly had such a strong feeling of foreboding when I looked up at that house."

"The cottage frightened you?"

"When I looked up at it, I realized how grand it once must have been and what the years had done to it. Have you ever read any of Shirley Jackson's work?"

"Sure, I love horror stories. 'The Lottery', *The Haunting of Hill House*."

"She's one of my favorite authors."

"They just made a movie out of her novel, *We Have Always Lived in This Castle*. I know the director Stacie Passon. Sunny almost got me a tryout for the part of Uncle Julian."

"I saw the movie. They cast Cristian Glover but you would have been great in that role."

"You were always my biggest fan."

"I went alone to see it. I didn't stay for the whole movie. I left when Merricat said to Constance, 'The world is full of terrible people.' I ran out of the theatre and sat in my car and locked the doors."

"Do you want me to tell you how it ends?"

"Somehow I think I'd rather not know. We've come so far away from the dreamers we were in those days. I wish …."

"So, I guess you won't be putting a bid on the Browning cottage?"

"Whoever does buy it must realize, it won't be there forever. It might not make it through the next storm. We might not make it through the next storm. Nothing is promised to any of us." She began to cry.

Elliot put his arm around her. "Okay, listen to me, nothing's going to hurt you. Ever again." He brushed his fingertips against the tears on her face.

"Promise?"

"I promise. Now, since I've decided to return to New York tonight, let's find something fun to do for the rest of the time we have together. Since we won't be buying that old Victorian, we just saved ourselves a million dollars. Let's splurge. We can start by going around the corner to the Oyster Bar for some jumbo shrimp, then Italian caviar and a dozen oysters, followed by a couple of stuffed lobsters, and we'll wash it all down with a bottle of champagne to celebrate the good news that you are no longer the prime suspect.'"

"*Veuve Clicquot*?"

"Whatever your heart desires."

"You had me at jumbo shrimp. Truly a meal fit for a king."

"And his queen."

"Then lead on McDuff."

⍥

Sergeant Shwinnard stopped by Belmont's at noon to pick up a few staples to get him through the next few days. "You can never have enough spam in your cupboard when a storm is looming on the horizon," he informed the people around him at the checkout. This pearl of wisdom elicited a few dubious looks and one victory sign from a teenage bagger who happened to be a *Monty Python* fan.

The sergeant had been busy most of the morning going to houses along the shore seeing if anyone might need transportation out of the area. One lady, Mrs. Chumsley, refused to leave her dog. Her daughter had allergies and informed her mother that she couldn't bring him with her. Sergeant Shwinnard promised if she would go with him to her daughter's house, he would take care of her pet. He helped the woman pack an overnight bag for herself and one for Trini.

When he'd dropped the woman off at her daughter's place, he continued on his rounds. Trini Lopez Chumsley was perfectly happy to sit in the passenger seat keeping his new best friend company. The sergeant even turned on the siren and the animal hung out of the squad car howling along as they traveled up and down the coastline looking for people who might need assistance in evacuating.

They arrived at the Safety Complex and Shwinnard placed Trini's doggy bed in a quiet corner of his office where the dog promptly fell asleep with his favorite toy tucked under his chin. Shwinnard went out to the dispatcher's office. "Leo, have you seen Detective Sullivan?"

"He called and said he'd be back here within the hour."

"Any other news?"

"The storm hasn't even hit yet and already a tree has come down on the wires at the corner of Broad Rock and Saugatucket. I've sent a police car. Power's out and a crew's been called in. Looks like they won't have power any time soon."

"Okay, I'll head over later to see if anyone in the neighborhood needs a ride to the shelter."

When Sullivan returned, he found the sergeant sharing his spam sandwich with a rather ratty looking Chihuahua. "Hey, looks like you've got yourself another partner. So how was your day so far?"

"People have begun leaving the beach front. Most of the houses are rentals and closed for the season, so it wasn't much of a problem, except for Trini's mom and one old guy who said he wouldn't leave, 'Come hell or high water'. I'm planning on going back later to check on him. How was your day so far?"

"My cousin Gerry asked me to follow up on a tip regarding the Duckworth case. You know that he has Rick Carnavale in custody but a woman, who didn't identify herself, called and said he's nabbed the wrong guy and should speak with Elliot Scott. It seems the victim, Morgan Duckworth, attended one of his performances last week and afterwards, this witness overheard them having an argument out on the beach."

"Did you find out anything useful?"

"I went out to the theatre this morning and it was deserted. I spoke with the owner of the house Elliot Scott was renting and she said as far as she knew, he'd returned to New York. He's not answering at the cell phone number he gave Gerry."

"What's his connection to the victim?"

"Gerry said Scott admitted to having a past relationship with Morgan Duckworth but left out the part that he'd seen her recently. He stated he hadn't communicated with her in years."

"Exactly. The night she was killed, he was on stage and then he says afterwards he went to the cabaret in the restaurant. I think the Narragansett police are going to have to dig a little further to see if this holds up. The performance ended at 10:30 and Morgan was run down just after 11:00. He certainly could have had time, if his alibi doesn't hold up."

"He gave names of people who supposedly saw him at the post performance. Gerry's a little worried he may have moved too quickly on the arrest. He needs to bring Scott back in after he narrows down the last time he was seen. The cabaret ended around one in the morning."

"If Scott never arrived back in New York, he could still be in South County. It's strange about the cell phone, though. Actors are always waiting for a call from their agents regarding work. I can't imagine one turning off his phone."

"My guess is he has caller ID and is just not answering certain calls. I told Gerry I'd help him with anything here in South Kingstown. He's following up on some other leads. Can you hold down the fort for me until I get back? Jess wants me to pick up some milk and bread and snacks."

"Good luck with that. We assigned personnel to the local supermarkets this morning directing traffic in and out of the parking lots. I'm sure the shelves are all empty by now. But I may be able to help. I made some cookies last night." Opening his bottom desk drawer, he took out a box, which he handed to Carl who opened it and sniffed.

"Chocolate chip. My favorite. Thanks. The boys will love them. Who needs bread when you can eat cookies?"

CR

The labradoodles ran from the back of the house when they heard the car pull up the drive. Kara planned to arrive a little earlier to be there to introduce Sophia to Lenore. The Curies were curious about the bundle she carried onto the porch. The door opened before she could ring the bell. She stepped inside and let Lenore take the baby carrier with her into the study where she placed it on the couch next to her. The dogs sat up expectantly at her feet.

"Marie and Pierre Curie, I would like you to meet Miss Celia Langley." Lenore announced.

Celia's eyes grew wide as she was tipped forward a bit for a better view of the strange new animals staring up at her. She gurgled, waving her hands and wiggling her feet. They barked back a greeting which startled her for a moment. She looked to her mother for assurance that she had nothing to fear from the strange creatures and smiled when Kara knelt between the dogs to pet their heads and they jumped up and wagged their tails.

"What playful puppies, Celia! Wait 'til your Aunt Sophia gets here. She'll want to take a picture of you with your new friends." To Lenore she added, "Sophia thinks Celia should have a pet. She's a pediatric nurse and has some set ideas on the best ways to bring up a child in this day and age."

Just then the doorbell rang and Lenore called out, "The door's open, come right in."

Kara stood to make the introduction. "I'd like you to meet my friend Sophia." She was wearing a bright yellow woolen cape with a navy turtle-neck, matching trousers and navy suede ankle boots. Lenore nodded and Sophia gave the room an appreciative once over.

"Your house is impressive. I've never been inside any of the mansions along the ocean on this side of the Bay. I always wondered what it was like beyond the black iron gates and hedges."

"I'll show you around, if you'd like. Before you start packing up the wardrobe."

"I'd like that. Let me just go back out to the car and bring in the storage boxes. I have an idea for a fundraiser to benefit the children's ward at the hospital. I could get other women to donate the designer clothes I'm sure they have lying around in their closets. We could plan a luncheon with a fashion show at the Dunes Club. And you'll be my guest of honor." She ran outside.

"She truly is a whirlwind with a marvelous sense of style."

"Sophia makes her own clothes. She was a model in New York City while she was working her way through nursing school."

"Nursing school in New York? I wonder if she ever met Morgan?"

Sophia came back with boxes. The car keys were dangling from her mouth. "I'm afraid I don't have any pockets." She placed them on one of the hooks on the wall just inside the entryway. "I'll get them when I leave. This is convenient. I'll have to have Gino put some hooks by our front door. I'm always misplacing my keys."

"I can sympathize. I have the same problem. That was my husband's idea. It saved us from being late on many occasions. He died. I miss him terribly. And now Morgan is gone, too ..."

"I was sorry to hear of your daughter's death. It must have been quite a shock for you."

Lenore acted as if she hadn't heard Sophia's offer of condolence. "Kara tells me you studied to be a nurse in New York. Did you know my daughter Dr. Morgan Duckworth?"

Sophia hesitated and looked at Kara. "I did recognize her name from a medical conference I attended. Morgan may have been on the program as a presenter."

"Oh, I doubt that. I'm sure there must have been doctors far better qualified to speak at a conference than my daughter. Well, let me show you around this mausoleum before you start to work." Sophia gave Kara a knowing glance.

She saved her daughter's room for last and opened the doors to the walk-in closet. Sophia gasped at the collection of designer shoes along one side. She walked the length of the wall touching each one as though it was a holy relic.

"What size are you, dear?"

"Seven and a half," Sophia answered wistfully.

"I think that's the same size as Morgan's. Please choose the ones you'd like to keep. Unfortunately, I'm much smaller than she was and my shoe size is a five. She favored her father's side of the family. He was a tall, handsome man. And we certainly didn't have the same taste in shoes at all. I've never worn a sandal in my life. I found it appalling that a doctor would wear such high heels. Studies have shown it throws off your body alignment and causes many problems when you're my age. I've always worn sensible shoes." She didn't notice that Sophia was in a trance and didn't hear anything she had to say after the words, "…choose the ones you'd like …".

"And here's something for you, Kara." She pointed to a package on the bed, taking the baby from her mother's arms so her hands were free to unwrap it. Inside was a soft, blue sweater, folded neatly in tissue paper. "Morgan never wore this. She wasn't one to wear pastels. But it will look lovely against your dark skin. It's made of alpaca fleece. Someone gave it to her as a gift. I found it in her bureau, still in the box. When I tried to get her to wear it, she said she was saving it for best and laughed. Morgan saved nothing. She felt that everything she did was the best. It was a favorite joke of her father's and mine when she was younger."

Kara held up the sweater and felt the rich, thick, ply. "Thank you Lenore. It's lovely."

"And now we'll go up to the nursery and Celia can choose a gift for herself."

Sophia was unwilling to leave the outfits surrounding her and called out from the closet, "You go ahead, I think I'll just stay here and begin to sort through these clothes."

A servant's stairway from the kitchen led to the third floor where two suites of rooms were separated by pocket doors.

"I redesigned part of the old nursery into an apartment for me to stay when I choose to come home for a visit." A cozy bedroom and sitting room with an attached bathroom took up half of the space. Lenore slid open the set of doors revealing a child's bedroom on the other side with a crib, a rocking chair, a twin bed, two bureaus and a large wardrobe. A Teddy bear riding a rocking horse was tucked under an eave and next to it was a brightly painted play kitchen "My two girls spent endless hours pretending to prepare meals. My husband had it specially made for them," she added.

Sunlight coming from a window-paned door warmed the stuffed animals clustered together on the bed. Outside the door was a balcony with an ornately carved railing along its front. Kara walked toward the light.

"Oh, please don't take the baby out there! Please, Morgan!" Lenore cried out.

Kara heard the alarm in her voice. She turned and brought Celia over to the bed, filled to the brim with plush toys. Lenore appeared relieved. She joined them and began to pick the stuffed animals up, one by one, rubbing first a tiny white terrycloth bunny, then a pink angora kitten under the baby's chin, tickling her and making her smile.

"They're all perfectly safe for an infant. I had Nanny Green remove any ribbons and adornments. Choking hazards, you know. Nanny replaced button eyes and noses with brightly colored exes sewed on with the finest silk embroidery thread. It's important we keep our children safe." Placing a well-worn, black velveteen puppy with loppy ears next to her heart, she said to Celia, "This was my Angela's favorite toy of all."

Celia didn't appear to be impressed with the puppy nor any of the other stuffed toys held up for her approval. Her attention seemed to focus in the direction of the rocking horse.

"Is it the Teddy bear you like, Darling?' Kara asked. "Let's go see." But it wasn't the bear she was interested in. It was the kitchen set. She shook her fists with glee when her mother bent down and opened the wooden refrigerator stocked with play food. And she crowed happily as Lenore placed a pot on the stove top and pretended to add soup and stir it with a child-size ladle.

"I think this is her choice, although it seems a strange one for an infant," Lenore commented handing Celia the wooden utensil which the gleeful baby immediately began to chew.

Kara laughed. "My husband will be overjoyed. He loves to cook."

"Well, I'll hold Celia while you move it down to your car."

"It's lucky I drove the SUV, today."

On one of her trips down the stairs, Kara looked in on Sophia. "How's it going?"

"Good, so far. I may have to come back with Gino at a later time, though. This closet goes on forever. And I thought I had the best collection of designer shoes in town. Look at these *Mephisto Lissandra* sandals." She handed them to Kara with reverence. Sophia was in seventh heaven.

Kara handed them back. She was not impressed. "Well, I'll leave you to it, then. Make sure you take all of the shoes in the first trip."

"That's a given. Did Celia make a choice?"

"Yes, she did. A mini kitchen set," Kara informed her.

"That girl is definitely her father's child," Sophia declared.

"I'll help you when you're ready to load these boxes into the car. The sun just went behind some clouds when I was outside just now. Looks like rain."

"I'll get a move on, then," Sophia said.

The first of the rains came as they closed Sophia's car and returned to the warmth of the drawing room where Lenore was coaxing the Curies to entertain Celia with tricks. First Marie would roll over followed by Pierre. It was a happy little tableau.

Kara sat down but Sophia remained standing. "I want to get a picture of Celia with the dogs and then I'm afraid I'll need to leave to get to the hospital in time. " She snapped some photos with her cell phone. "Before I forget, I found a box of chocolates with a card made out to you on one of the shelves in the closet. It's on the bureau next to items I emptied from the pockets. Thank you, Lenore, I know the hospital will benefit from your generosity. I'll see you at your house later tonight," she called out to Kara as she left.

They sat comfortably chatting for an hour. The baby was fed and had fallen asleep in her carrier on the couch. "Lenore, would you like to come home with us? You can bring Marie and Pierre. The three of you could share the guest room. Stewart is making a crock-pot of stew. Comfort food."

"No, Dear. I'm expecting a call from my lawyer. Besides, I haven't been eating much lately. I have no appetite. I think I'll go find that box of candy, though. There's always room for chocolate."

"Please phone if you need anything. You're welcome at our house any time. Celia will cook for you. Pretend food. Very few calories."

"I'll be fine. I'm sure the weathermen are getting everyone riled up and it will end up being just another false alarm. I've survived many storms in this old house. If I need to go anywhere I can always call for a ride."

Lenore waved at them from the front door. Kara suddenly felt a sharp sense of dread. She'd wanted to stay longer, but the rain had begun to come down in earnest and she had a strong need to hug Stewart and feel the comfort of her own home. In the weeks to follow, Kara would remember this moment vividly - the smiling woman on the porch with Pierre and Marie sitting up staunchly on either side of her like loyal guard dogs. In the weeks to follow, she would look back and remember this moment with sadness.

෪

Selina and Elliot left the restaurant and decided to take a ride around the local villages before he had to return to the cottage to get ready for his trip back to the city. She drove along pointing out some of her favorite old buildings and places. Suddenly, she made a sharp right turn which led up a long cement drive ending in front of the house with a circular turn-around and a fountain with a sculpture in the middle. "So, this is where I'll be staying for the winter." She jumped out to look at the house.

He stood next to her admiring the architecture.

"The first time I ever saw this place, I thought it was a castle. Those incredible turrets and the rounded beveled windows. I was sure a princess lived up in that room." She pointed to the west window with its balcony overhanging the front yard. It didn't seem to bother her that they were getting soaked.

"Is that your work?" Elliot nodded toward the sculpture in the middle of the fountain.

"Yes, it was the first piece commissioned after I left the hospital." She moved toward it and he followed.

It reminded him of Rodin's *The Kiss* - two figures locked in an embrace. But this statue had three figures, a woman behind the two lovers silently watching. He circled around it in the rain marveling at the workmanship. "I think this is one of your best, Selina. It's magnificent." He bent to look at the base. *La Trahison* was etched into the metal plaque. "What does *trahison* … ?"

The question was left unfinished as Selina shed her sweater and stepped over the stone wall into the island of water surrounding the sculpture.

"Selina, you're sopping wet! We need to get you inside and dried off."

She laughed and stood on the edge of the fountain. Leaning over precariously, she touched the face of the watching woman. Just below the right eye was a tiny tear rendered almost invisible by the streaks of water trickling down from the crown of curls atop the figure's head. Selina touched the teardrop and suddenly lost her balance falling into the shallow basin. Elliot jumped in and she splashed him as he pulled her out onto the drive and then under the cover of the front porch. She looked up into his eyes and he bent to kiss the top of her head. She took a key from her pocket. "Come on in. I'll give you the royal tour."

CB

15

Under the harvest moon,
When the soft silver
Drips shimmering
Over the gray mocker,
Comes and whispers to you
As a beautiful friend
Who remembers.

-Carl Sandburg, "Under the Harvest Moon"

There's a moon behind the clouds tonight. The Harvest moon - preparing for the autumnal equinox. Enough light for farmers to bring in the crops. To harvest the corn. I think I'm alone. No lights on in studios. Nobody working late on a Friday night. Friday the 13th. Someone keeps tapping on my walls. Outside in the hall. No one is there when I call out. Where is the crazy old man who seems to be around every corner? I have the feeling he's watching me. He reminds me of Grazio.

Elliot was curious about La Trahison. When I told finally told him it meant The Betrayal, he became so sad. He said he had something to tell me...

What is that tapping? Perhaps the mice are getting their nests ready for winter? I'm working on the last maquette. More and more I prefer working on miniatures. It gives me a feeling of power. Everything is so much smaller. I can control it. Fashion it all into how I want it to look. Mold it into memories. Precious memories. Bad memories. The world is full of terrible people.

Selina was jolted from a nightmare by a rapping at the doors to the studio. "Selina, it's Lynn. Are you in there?"

She jumped up to partially cover her miniature creation with a cloth before unbolting the doors. "Lynn, I must have drifted off." She looked out the window. "What time is it?"

"It's almost 9 o'clock, Selina. I had to bring keys to a new tenant this morning and thought I'd stop by to chat for a while. I saw your car out back. You're here early."

"It's morning? Excuse me. I'm sorry to keep you standing in the hall. Come in. I can put on some chamomile tea if you'd like."

"That would be nice. Oh, your castle came out wonderful."

Selina turned on a light behind the sculpture making it appear transparent.

"What a stunning effect!" Do you have a buyer?"

Selina filled an earthenware teapot with water and placed it in the microwave. "No, this is one I'm going to give as a gift."

"What are you working on now?" Lynn moved to the table and peeked under the cloth. "This looks kind of like a diorama. We used shoeboxes to make them when we were in school. We'd re-create favorite scenes from books or from events in history."

"It's a scale model. A maquette. I've been doing a series of them. I'm just starting that one."

"Will you be making them into life-sized sculptures?"

"No." A ping signaled the water had reached its boiling point. She dropped in loose tea leaves in a small mesh bag to brew and tucked the pot into a woven tea cozy, setting it on a table in front of the couch. "Please come in here and sit."

"I recognize this." Lynn picked up the colorful woven bowl. "It's one of the pieces from Dragon Fiber Arts. Kathryn's designs are unique."

"Yes, and I bought the mugs from the potter in 109 and the hand-made journals come from Kelly in 201. I've tried to buy something from each of the artists, except for the old man who roams around the corridors. I haven't been able to find his studio."

"Oh, that sounds like Esbon Sanford. He was the original owner of the mill. He doesn't have a studio. He's one of our spirits," Lynn informed her as she sipped carefully, testing the temperature.

"You mean a ghost?"

"Yes, we have a few. Have you met the General? Or maybe Byron Gideon? Byron's not old. As a matter of fact, he's only 18. He was one of the southerners – the prisoners of war, locked in the cells under Fort Adams. They let some of them out to work in the mills during the Civil War. His name is carved into the original wallboards in Room 209. Right next door. He never went back down south in the end. He liked it here."

"I've been having dreams - nightmares about people who don't ever talk. They just stare at me like they're waiting - expecting something."

"Our spirits have been here for a long time. They're all quite harmless. The worst they do is move stuff around, but they always bring back the things they borrow. Have you heard the children?"

"I hear children playing all the time late into the night. Little girls singing."

"That would be the children who came here with their mothers to make the material to clothe sharecroppers and miners back in the early days. And of course there's John and Mary. They sing, too, and they like to waltz together on the stage in 200."

"I bought some beautiful embroidered pieces from the woman in that studio. I didn't see any ghosts, though. I got a peaceful feeling while I was there. What was the mill before it became an artists' colony?"

"It's always been a special place. My father bought it at auction in 1955. King Fastener Company, he named it. We manufactured metal staples and machines for over thirty years. He hired me to pack staples into boxes in the summers when I was a teenager. I often think about the women who worked here then. I realized when I was older how special they were. They kept their families fed and clothed."

"I remember you telling me about your father the first time I came to see the studios. He's the one who started the transformation, turning the mill into a place for artisans to work."

"Artists would pick their space and measure it by the number of windows and then my dad would make a mark and a wall was built. These walls have seen so much history. It's filled with memories and spirits, of course. I never thought to ask - are you afraid of ghosts?"

"Just the ones haunting my own dreams, although I think I fear the living more."

"Well, I thank you for the tea and the conversation. I have to check back to see how our new artist is settling in and then I must stop on my way home to get some milk and bread. Stay safe."

After Lynn left, Selina took the maquette and gingerly placed it into the bottom of the old hope chest with the others. She looked for her latest journal, but it wasn't on the desk where she'd left it the night before. She searched and found it on one of the seats in the sandbox. She placed it in her bag, turned off the lights, locked up, and started for home. The smell of storm was in the air.

CB

16

I feel we are all islands in a common sea.
-Anne Morrow Lindbergh, *Gift from the Sea*

THE EVACUATION TEAM HAD spent most of the previous Saturday night and the early Sunday morning hours making sure everyone along the coastline and the flood zones had transportation and a place to stay. Sergeant Shwinnard returned to the few homes where people had refused to leave. He tried to reason with them. He was on his way to old Mr. Carpenter's place when a call came in from the station.

"Sarge, it's Leo. How's it going out there?"

"Trini and I are almost done. I've got one more stop."

"Make that two. We had a call from the Narragansett station. It seems a guy named Elliot Scott's gone missing. His fiancée in New York has been trying to contact him since Friday. He never made it home. She's frantic because she hasn't been able to reach him on his cell. I might add, he's a person of interest in the Morgan hit and run."

"I'm familiar with the situation. He's an actor. I took my wife to see him in *Chicago* in August here in Matunuck."

"That's the guy. Detective Sullivan wants you to go by the place he rented while he was in town and maybe check out the theatre. See if you can find out if he's been there in the last few days."

"Will do. Give me the address and I'll get back to you with what I find out."

He looked into the back seat where Trini was gazing back at him in the rear-view mirror. "How would you like it if I turned the siren on?"

Trini stuck out his tongue.

"I'll take that as a yes."

They headed toward Cards Pond Road with the red light flashing and Trini singing along with the siren.

cs

"I'll answer the phone if you take care of changing Celia's diaper."

"Sounds like I'm getting the raw end of the deal," Stewart informed his wife.

"Kara, it's Gerry Sullivan. Is this an inconvenient time?"

"Actually, your timing is perfect."

"I'd like to fill you in on what's been happening with the Duckworth case. I know you feel I shouldn't have jumped so fast in arresting your friend. But we matched the tire track at the Duckworth estate to the one on the cab he was driving that night. He was there and he didn't tell us. He's still closed mouth about the whole thing."

"Gerry, you should know I'm working to prove that Rick was not the killer."

"I know, Kara. And that's why I'm calling you. We released him on bail this morning. And one of the other suspects has disappeared. Elliot Scott, the actor. Selina Borelli's ex."

"I recognize that name."

"His girlfriend's been frantic - calling us since Saturday morning. He left New York City on Thursday and was expected to return on Saturday. But he never made it home. He told her he was meeting an old friend he was helping out with a problem and would be back in time for dinner on Saturday. They had plans to go out with friends to celebrate their engagement. She's positive he wouldn't have missed it unless something is really wrong."

"Was he a prime suspect?"

"We figure he had a motive. He hated Morgan for breaking up his marriage. And come to find out, he had the opportunity. We wanted to bring him in to question him about lying to us in his statement. He said he was at the cabaret after the show the night Duckworth was killed. But witnesses say he wasn't. He left the theatre right after the performance."

"How reliable are the witnesses?"

"The bartender, waiters, other actors. Somebody should have seen him. We want to find out why he lied. And he told us he'd had no contact with the victim while he was here in RI. But one of the waitresses recognized Morgan's picture from the newspaper and remembered seeing him arguing with her the week before she was murdered. They were on the beach after one of the matinees and the conversation became quite heated. She slapped him in the face and he grabbed her arm. Now that he's suddenly disappeared, it doesn't look good for him."

"I have to agree. Maybe Selina can give you a lead on Elliot?"

"We're calling her back in as soon as she answers the messages I've left on her cell phone. And I'm still working on tracking down the second check sent to Carnavale."

"What was the check for?"

"It appears Morgan was trying to ease her conscience in regard to his wife's death. She wasn't at her store, when he showed up, but he left a message with her business partner that he didn't want the money. He says he ripped up the check."

"Thanks, Gerry. I know you arrested the wrong person, but I'm glad you're continuing to look at information you receive on the case. That's the sign of a good detective. Your cousin Carl always kept an open mind."

"He said the same thing about you. I appreciated the help you gave us on the victim's mother. Have you heard anything from Mrs. Duckworth lately?"

"Not since I went to the house to help with Morgan's things."

"After my first conversation with her, I felt she could have been a suspect. I found her relationship with her daughter to be strange."

"I saw some animosity there, too, when we spoke. But I don't seriously think she'd run down her own daughter. There's no real motive. She owned the property and the business and she controlled the money. It would have been more likely for Morgan to kill her mother."

"It was probably wise that she moved out, then. I'll let you go. If you hear anything about Scott, please give me a call."

"Take care, Gerry."

Stewart came into the kitchen with Celia. He took her to the little play kitchen. "Now for your very first cooking lesson."

"What have you decided is on the menu this morning?" Kara asked.

To his daughter he said, "I was thinking we would treat your mommy to my famous Blue Moon pancakes."

"Yummy," Kara said rolling her eyes.

Celia drooled.

"I thought you'd both be impressed."

ᚑᛋ

Lenore had phoned Selina on Sunday and left a message asking her to stop by. "I've moved back to Ocean Road. I'd love a visit if you have some time."

Selina called her on Monday morning to say she'd be there at noon and asked if she needed anything.

"I'm fine. Pat came by with groceries, so I can make us lunch, if you'd like."

"I'll bring us something for dessert," Selina said.

"Something chocolate, please."

She listened to the weather on her car radio. The hurricane had stalled off the coast of Maryland but was definitely headed toward RI once it started up again. The wind gusts had already brought tree limbs down and trucks were out making sure the roads stayed clear. She would stay with Lenore for a short time and go back to the mill to work on her project.

Lenore was happy to see her. "I know you don't have a lot of time, so we'll skip *hors d'ouevres*."

Selina handed her a package and she peeked inside. "You brought cake!"

"It's from Gregg's."

"My favorite. Death by Chocolate." She took pills from the *Limoges* case. She poured the wine and washed down her pills.

"The table looks exquisite, Lenore. I love this china set and your *Waterford* crystal. But it's only lunch. Shouldn't you be saving it for a more formal dinner? For best as you've always told me the nanny would say?"

"Morgan hated it when Nanny would tell her to put a gift away for best. She'd sneak into her closet and dress up in her newest clothes and then come down for school just to make a point. When I think of the outfits she used to go out to play in. The other children must have thought she was quite the little snob."

"I don't think she much cared what other people thought of her," Selina said.

"Her father and I always worried about her. The psychiatrists told us to take care of her self-esteem. As I look back, that was the very least of our worries."

"Yes, she had a strong feeling of entitlement."

"I'm so sorry about what happened to you, Leena. I've been wanting to have this talk with you and now that Morgan's gone, it's time. You see, I realize everything that happened was partially my fault because I never made her try to look at things from other people's point of view. She had no empathy. I should have seen it and not been so adamant about her becoming a doctor. I thought she would learn to care, be sympathetic. I believed she would be a better human being if she could help heal people's suffering."

"Narcissists never see beyond their own needs. I wish I'd never met her. She ruined my life. I look back and wonder where I'd be today if we'd never met."

"I'd hoped you and Yvonne could be role models to help her to become less self- absorbed. I admit I was wrong. Nothing could have helped her."

"You always blamed her behavior on the accident. On Angela's death."

"I never told anyone the truth about what happened that day. If I had, then everything would have been different for all of us."

"What do you mean?"

"Morgan was not outside playing that day. We were all in the nursery. I'd sent Nanny Green on an errand. Morgan was angry because the baby was taking up my time. She wasn't feeling well. She had a fever and I was trying to rock her to sleep. Morgan wanted me to play with her. I left the two girls and went into the bathroom to get Angela some medicine and when I came out, Morgan was standing on the balcony looking down at Angela on the grass below. I've always kept that a secret from everyone, even her father. It was a mistake. I know that now. I'm sorry, Selina. You were just another one of Morgan's victims. Like Grazio and Evie. But at least you're still alive. She was never sorry for any hurt she caused. I believe it's better that she's gone. She was evil. There was no saving her. It know now that it would have been better for so many people if she'd died sooner."

Selina sat upright in her chair, stunned into silence by what Lenore was sharing with her as she went on about her daughter and the pain she had caused. *Yet another betrayal by someone I thought loved me. She told everyone she considered me her other daughter. She used me like Elliot did. I wanted him to stay with me. I pleaded with him. I told him I was sick and still, he told me he needed to leave to be with her. I have no one I can trust. I never had anyone. The world truly is filled with terrible people.*

"I'll just be a minute." Lenore left the room and returned with the cake.

"Selina, can I pour you more wine? Are you finished with your meal?"

"No, thank you Lenore. I've had enough." She stood up suddenly. "I have to be going."

"What about dessert?"

"I have to go."

Lenore called after her as she ran out the door. "I'll just put the cake away and we'll save it for later." She poured herself another glass of wine and took it into the library.

CB

Sergeant Shwinnard sat in Rolly Carpenter's front room drinking hot apple cider on a scratchy, horsehair couch. Trini lay at the old man's feet. Rolly was glad for the company and his new friends proved an appreciative audience as he related stories of his life in South Kingstown.

"My family's been living in Matunuck for generations. That grist mill next door was built in 1716 by James Perry and they moved it here to Moonstone Beach Road around about 1789. People loved to move entire buildings back in those days. The bigger the better. None of this tearing places down to make way for modern eyesores like they do today. When's the last time you came across such a sturdy post and beam structure? The older generation, like me and my parents, appreciated a good piece of architecture when they saw it. It's one of the oldest corn mills in the state. Before 1860, the corn used to be ground between two stone wheels, now it's a turbine that does the work. The water from the pond runs through to help create a fine whitecap flint powder. And when you fry that corn flour up, you get the finest Johnny cakes you'd ever want to eat. My family ran the mill from the 1870s through the 1960s," he said proudly. "Would you like me to fry you up some Johnny cakes?"

Shwinnard took advantage of the break in Rolly's narrative. "That certainly is an offer I would like to take you up on some time, but the wind seems to be blowing louder outside. I brought along something I thought you might like to look at." The sergeant handed a book to the old man. It had photographs of the destruction left behind by the various storms over the years.

"Oh, my parents used to tell me about the 1938 hurricane. The Yankee Clipper they called it. We lived in town at the time. I was a little tyke. Eighteen to twenty-five-foot tides. They were higher than usual because of the fall equinox and the full moon."

"The storm surge was really bad here in Rhode Island." Shwinnard pointed to pictures of summer cottages floating in the ocean. "So many beach communities were washed out to sea." He watched as Carpenter turned the pages and scanned the pictures of Napatree Point and the ones of Downtown Providence under water. "You can see how high the water level was on a plaque at the Old Market House. The surge from the Providence River was powerful. People drowned in their cars. Whale Rock Lighthouse, at the entrance of Narragansett Bay in South County, was swept away. The lighthouse keeper's body was never found." The sergeant was hoping he was making his point, but the old man wasn't convinced. "They figure about 800 people died just here in Rhode Island. You don't mess around with Mother Nature."

"That was back in the days they didn't give 'em names. Today they even have boys' names. I gotta say, I like the girls' names better. Carol, Donna, Gloria ... Bob and Bill just don't make it in my book."

"I know you want to make sure everything's okay around here but I was wondering if you could help me with something?"

"What can I do for you?"

"I need to go to Card's Pond Road. I'm looking for someone who's disappeared. Maybe you could take a ride with me and Trini?"

"Okay, it's close by. As long as you bring me back when we're done. I've got to keep an eye on the old grist mill, so don't get any ideas about kidnapping me."

"It's a deal. And you can tell me some more of your stories while we're riding around. Trini's a good companion but he isn't much of a conversationalist." The dog tilted his head and howled.

"I think you might have hurt his feelings. We should let him sit in the front seat," Rolly suggested as he put on his duffel coat and they started out on their adventure.

The theatre was boarded up as they walked around looking for a way to gain entrance. "I used to usher here when my friend Tommy Brent owned the place. I got to see lots of shows. Some were weird like that *Sweeney Todd* Demon Barber musical. I had nightmares for months and you still won't get me to eat a meat pie. Not if my life depended on it! I preferred the old musicals like *Mame* and *No, No, Nanette*. But I got in for free and beggars can't be choosers."

"It looks like there's no one here. We'll just go over to the restaurant and be on our way." Shwinnard called the number of the property management company on the posted sign outside of the building. He spoke with a woman who assured him everyone had been long gone. He asked about Elliot Scott and she told him he'd left for New York then gave him the number of his cell phone.

Shwinnard walked around the property dialing the number and listening to see if he could hear a ring tone over the screeching of the seagulls and the smashing of the waves. "I've got one more place to go and then I'll get you on home."

The door was unlocked. They called inside but no one answered so they let themselves in. Shwinnard went into the kitchen and dialed the cell phone number. The sound of music came from the couch. Carpenter rushed over and began to lift up the cushions.

"That tune sounds familiar. I think it's from the last musical they did here this season. 'Mr. Cellophane'. The guy who played the part was really good. Elliot Scott. Here it is." He held the phone up and then handed it to the Sergeant."

"I gotta get this back to the station, pronto. Maybe it will help them figure out where this guy's disappeared to. You've been a big help, Rolly."

"Maybe I should go with you? In case you need another set of ears or someone to lend a hand."

"That's a good idea. And it's almost time for lunch."

The old man had tucked Trini inside his coat and the dog poked out his head when he heard the word lunch. "I think he's hungry."

"I got some sandwiches back at the station. He loves deviled ham."

"Spam! Who doesn't love spam?" Rolly smacked his lips. "Ummm, ummmm!"

Trini yipped happily, wagged his tail, and burrowed his head back into the warm woolen shelter as the three amigos headed back into town.

ভ

17

Listen! You hear the grating roar
Of pebbles which the waves draw back, and fling,
At their return, up the high strand,
Begin, and cease, and then again begin,
With tremulous cadence slow and bring
The eternal note of sadness in.

-Matthew Arnold, "Dover Beach"

B Y THE TIME IT had reached the coast of Rhode Island on Wednesday, the hurricane officially had worn itself down to a tropical storm. It continued to rage throughout the night and into the next morning and then it finally began to move farther out to sea.

Teams from the Narragansett Electric Company were out in force assessing damage to power lines and setting priorities for restoring service. Kara began making calls to check on friends. Although Stewart had to reset the clocks, they'd only experienced a few flickers and had not lost power. She offered their spare room, a meal, and a hot shower to anyone who had not been so fortunate.

The college was closed so Ruth said she'd be taking Kara up on her offer. She was coming over later on for lunch.

"Rick's going to clean up the downed limbs with some of the neighbors. Gino offered to help him and Sophia's filling in at the hospital for people who couldn't make it in for their shifts," Ruth informed her friend. "I'll be over in a while. I'm tired of hanging out in front of the fireplace.

Three days without power and I'm at my wits end. I was not made to be a pioneer woman."

When Kara told Stewart what was going on, he decided to get his gas-powered chain saw and help with the cleanup effort. Kara was glad to have a chance to talk with Ruth without the others around. She didn't have much to tell her, but wanted her to know she was working on getting evidence to help Rick clear his name.

CB

Ruth arrived, dropping two large bags on the counter. "From our refrigerator. It's only going to go bad so we might just as well have a feast. And my laundry is out in the car. I'll be right back." She returned with a clothes basket filled to the brim.

Kara said, "The bath water's running and I put out some of that lavender soap and bath bubbles you like so much. Oh, and there's a glass of pinot grigio by the tub. Take your time. We have nowhere to go and nothing to do."

Ruth gave her a hug. "Hot water. I may stay in there for hours! I'll just put these in the washer."

The phone rang. "Kara this is Sophia. I have some bad news. Lenore Duckworth is in the hospital. One of her friends found her unconscious this morning and called the rescue."

"Do you have any idea what happened to her? She seemed fine when we were there last week."

"I heard them say they were treating it as an overdose. Kara, it doesn't look good. I'll call you when I get more information."

Kara prepared lunch and the sandwiches and soup were on the table when Ruth came into the kitchen an hour later. "If I'd brought a book with me, I would have stayed in there soaking for the whole day. Thanks, I feel ten times better now. Oooh. And what is this?"

"It's Celia's very own kitchen set. A gift from Lenore," Kara explained.

"Has Stewart started giving her cooking lessons, yet?"

"She helped make breakfast this morning."

"I hope it wasn't anything blue." They both shared a knowing glance as they sat down at the table. "This is bringing back so many memories. When I was a kid, my mother always made tomato soup and grilled cheese for lunch whenever there was a storm. And butterscotch pudding with whipped cream and cocoa. And if we behaved, we were allowed to help her bake gingerbread for when my father came home. The smell of my mother's special gingerbread always made everyone feel all was going to be right with the world. Or at least in our little portion of the world."

"That was the go-to comfort food in our family, too. Only, our soup was *Campbell's* chicken noodle and our gingerbread was from a mix. I hope I can make good memories for Celia so when she grows up, she can share them with her best friend."

After lunch, they took their pudding and hot chocolate into the study and sat on the couch with their feet up on the coffee table.

"Sophia told me you went to the Duckworth house to help with Morgan's clothes. Did you learn anything more about the case?" Kara decided not to tell her about Rick's unaccounted time the night of the murder. She wanted to investigate it further and get his side of the story first. Instead she told Ruth some of what she'd learned from Gerry and Sophia latest news.

"It's taken a strange turn. One of the other suspects, Elliot Scott, has disappeared and Lenore Duckworth has been rushed to the hospital with an apparent overdose. Has Rick said anything to you?" Kara wondered how much Rick had shared.

"Nothing at all since our first conversation."

"Why don't you two have dinner here tonight and I'll get him aside and see what I can find out?"

"Good luck. Remember the first time you met him? You called him Chatty Cathy."

They both laughed.

"I think I may go to the hospital, if you'll watch Celia for me. And if you get bored, there's a new book in the local mystery series you like. It's on my night table. I'll just get it for you."

She returned with the book and wearing the new sweater Lenore had given her.

"That's beautiful on you, Kara. And it has pockets. Perfect! You love to gather up things as you move around."

Kara put her hands in the pocket and felt a piece a paper. She took it out. It was a check for $50,000 made out to Rick Carnavale. She hastily put it back. "I'll look in on Celia and see if she's awake." In the nursery, she carefully examined the check wondering how it got into the pocket of Morgan's sweater. Rick said he ripped it up. But Gerry told her there were two checks and this must be the second one. She needed to get some answers because this piece of evidence could place Rick at the scene and back in police custody.

She called in to Ruth before she left, "Celia's still asleep. Her bottle is in the fridge if she wakes up. I'll try not to be long."

⚃

Kara stopped by the pediatric ward to tell Sophia she was going to visit Lenore. Sophia promised to see her before she left for the day.

Gerry and a policewoman were outside Lenore's hospital room. He introduced the two women and told Kara, "Mrs. Duckworth's still unconscious. If she does wake up, they don't expect she'll be coherent. They did a tox test. It looks like she mixed drugs and alcohol."

"I'm just going to sit with her for a little while. My friend, Sophia is a nurse. I'll have her make sure they call you if Lenore wakes up."

"Thanks. We're still looking for Elliot Scott, but Carl had your Sergeant Shwinnard do some footwork for us and he found Scott's cell phone at Selina Borelli's cottage. We're running down leads, but it seems she's disappeared, too."

"You've got your hands full with this case, Gerry."

"Between that and the crazy weather, I haven't got a good night's sleep in a week. I spoke with my captain. Any help we can get from your end would still be appreciated."

She put her hand in the sweater pocket but didn't take the check out. She decided she would get to the bottom of this herself. Gerry had enough to do at the moment.

ርჳ

Kara sat by the side of the bed holding Lenore's hand. Sophia joined her and they spoke quietly.

"There hasn't been any change. The tox screen showed large doses of three drugs in her system. It wasn't an accident, Kara."

"I'd like to take a look around her house. Where are her things?"

"At the nurse's station in a cabinet. I'll see if the keys are there." She came back a few minutes later and handed Kara the keys. "These were in the pocket of the jacket she was wearing when they found her."

"Thanks. Ruth is at my house taking care of Celia. Let's meet there later on for dinner. I'll call Stewart and tell him to get something ready for everyone."

"Do you want me to go to Lenore's with you?"

"I won't be there very long and you've been working straight out for a couple of days. You must be exhausted. Go home and take a rest. I'll see you later at my place."

ርჳ

An eerie silence had fallen over the Duckworth home. The walls and floors seemed to echo with every sound like a mausoleum. Kara switched on the lights and hung the keys by the door.

On the table in the dining room were a thick lace tablecloth, a golden mum, and two silver candlesticks. The kitchen was neat and orderly with everything put away in its proper place. The beds were all made and clean towels hung in the bathrooms. The study was the only room that looked lived in. A fleece blanket lay in a heap on the floor in front of the couch. An opened box of chocolates was hidden under some magazines on the end table and a wine glass was tipped on its side. Kara took pictures with her cell phone and moved on to the next floor where the rooms were all in order. Morgan's bedroom had been emptied of any personal belongings.

The nursery was left as it had been when she'd last visited. She moved to the doors leading to the balcony overlooking the laurel hedge which separated the Duckworth estate from the one next door. Stepping outside, Kara could see a black car parked in the drive in front of the house. She returned and went to the bathroom. Inside the medicine cabinet were three amber colored pill containers. Two were completely full and the third was almost empty.

"What are you doing here?" a voice demanded.

Kara was momentarily startled. She'd made sure the door was locked when she'd come into the house. Selina was standing at the top of the stairs. She stepped forward into the room.

"I recognize you. You sat next to me at Lenore's luncheon."

"Yes, I remember you, too."

"I'm looking for Lenore. Do you know where she is?"

"She's in the hospital."

"The hospital? But I just saw her. Yesterday. She was fine. Did she fall?"

Kara didn't answer the question. "I'm here to pick up some clothes for her."

"Then she's all right. I thought something might be wrong when I didn't hear the dogs barking this morning."

"They're with a friend."

"Can she have visitors?"

"I would call first."

"Then I'll be leaving."

Kara waited until she heard the front door close before going downstairs and looking one more time around the first-floor rooms. She took the key from the hook and went outside to explore the property. At the end of the back lawn, rocky cliffs dropped off into the sea. The waves were still in a wild state, not fully exhausted by the storm. Sea spray came up and she closed her eyes taking a long drought of the fresh salt air swirling around her. She walked the perimeter between the two houses and when she came to an area with a sundial and a break in the hedge, she went through to the adjoining estate.

All the drapes were closed. She knocked on the front door although she didn't expect anyone to answer. The car was gone. She circled the fountain and then walked back across the grass to the Duckworth property. She phoned Gerry.

"Are you at the police station? I just spoke with Selina Borelli."

"What did she tell you?"

"She didn't have much to say. I'd like to talk to you. I can be at the station in a few minutes."

ɕʒ

Gerry was waiting in his office behind his desk, which was overflowing with paperwork. He stopped reading when she sat down.

"Now that is something I really don't miss," she said.

"And we're supposed to be in a paperless society? Have you gotten more information on the case?"

"Selina was at the Duckworth estate. I spoke with her, but I didn't mention anything to her about Elliot. I thought you would want to take the lead on that. I'm sure she must know where he's hiding out."

"You think he's in hiding? That would be great. One dead body is enough right now. Thanks for your help, Kara. I know why my cousin misses you so much. But our captain is glad you've been available to help us, We don't get many murders in this town."

"No problem. I've missed working with a team. But not enough to go back full time. If I find out anything else, I'll be in touch."

ɕʒ

18

And in the sweetness of friendship let there
be laughter, and sharing of pleasures.
For in the dew of little things the heart finds
its morning and is refreshed.

-Kahlil Gibran, *The Prophet*

EVERYONE WAS BUSY AT her house when she arrived. Gino and Rick waved at her from the lean-to on the side of the shed where they were stacking the wood they'd cut. Ruth and Celia were in the kitchen helping Stewart prepare dinner and Sophia was at the table with the Baby Langley binder in front of her busy writing the chapter about Celia's First Tropical Storm.

"Where have you been?" Sophia didn't wait for an answer. "Sit down. I have some questions for you. Here, fill in the answers on this sheet, please." Ruth chuckled and whispered something about Momma's homework in Celia's ear. Sophia shot her a warning glance.

Gino and Rick brought a box of wood into the living room just as Kara finished her assignment. Sophia added it into the pocket of the binder. They all helped to set the table in the dining room and Stewart announced that dinner was ready.

He began ladling beef stew into their bowls, and everyone breathed a collective sigh of relief because the broth was a healthy shade of brown. The doorbell rang and Gino jumped up to get it, returning with a large pizza box which he placed on the sideboard. "I thought we might need a back-up. Ya know, just in case ….” He grimaced, pointing to the tureen and sat back down. Sophia kicked him under the table. “Hey, whatsatfor?”

Ruth jumped in, “This stew is the best you’ve ever made, Stewart. I think it’s because Celia helped.”

They looked at the baby and clapped. She rewarded them with a burp and a smile.

The talk centered around storms they remembered from the past. They all recounted stories of where they’d been during the Blizzard of ’78. They ate the pizza for dessert and then helped to clear the table.

Everyone settled in for the night. Ruth and Stewart decided to binge watch the W. C. Fields’ movies; Gino went upstairs to take a hot shower; and Sophia announced she was exhausted and was going to bed with a book. Rick went into the kitchen and offered to hold Celia while Kara warmed up her bottle. They both smiled at the sound of their spouses’ laughter coming from the study. She handed him the bottle and he began to feed the baby. She sat down and waited for him to say something. Time passed and finally she said, “Rick, I know you would never hurt anyone. I know you didn’t kill Morgan.”

He looked at her. “I wanted to kill her, Kara. So I stayed as far away from her as possible, because I really couldn’t stand knowing she was alive and Evie was dead and I’d never see her again.”

“It’s been established you had motive, Rick, but they’re looking into whether you had the opportunity and you need to explain to me where you went the night of the accident and how this ended up at Morgan’s house?” She put the check in front of him and he stared at it as though it had legs and was crawling around the table.”

“Where did you get that?”

She didn’t answer.

“I’ve been worried they’d find it and … ”

“You know it would have been strong evidence you were at the scene.”

“Yes, I was there that night. The tread on the cab’s tire placed me outside the house, but the check …”

“I need you to tell me the whole story or I won’t be able to help you, Rick.”

"Morgan had been trying to reach me. She called and left messages. I texted that I wanted nothing to do with her. She showed up at the Arts Center and was asking for me. I avoided her. She was toxic and I didn't want her anywhere in my life. But when Morgan wanted something, she could be incredibly persistent."

"So, you're saying you never met with her?"

He was silent for a minute. "After the settlement with her other patients came through, she mailed me a check. I'd decided from the beginning I didn't want her money. It wouldn't bring Evie back or undo all of the terrible things she'd done to people."

"What did you do with the check?"

"I was furious. I brought it to her shop and ripped it up. She wasn't there, so I told the woman working behind the counter to tell Morgan she couldn't buy forgiveness."

"If you destroyed it then how do you explain this check? How did this end up at the Duckworth house?"

"The day of the accident, I received another check in the mail. A call came in to the cab company that night from the house. The caller asked specifically if I was on duty. They relayed the message to me that Lenore Duckworth had called asking for me to pick her up and they gave me the address. I'd dropped Lenore off that morning and she'd intended to stay the night, so it didn't seem strange that she would want a ride back to Sea View. When I got to the house, Morgan answered the door. I realized she'd made the call. She was always manipulative. I put the check on the entry table and left. I didn't say a word, but she stood screaming at me from the porch. She hated it when she didn't get what she wanted."

"What time was that?"

"About 9:45pm. It was logged into the book, so I could check the exact time."

"It was 9:49 to be exact." Kara let him know she'd checked it herself.

"I'll take your word for it."

"Where did you go after you left the Duckworth place?"

"I went to the Dunkin' Donuts across from Salt Pond Plaza. I got a coffee and took it over to the town beach."

"Do you think someone would remember seeing you?"

"I don't know. A kid waited on me. I gave this information to the police. They'll have found out who was working that night."

"Did anyone see you at the beach?" She didn't have hope for a witness at that time of night in the dark on a beach but asked anyway.

"I got out of the car and walked for a while. An old guy was there combing the sand with a metal detector. He spoke with me when I walked by."

"What did he look like?"

"He had a full beard, a handlebar mustache, bushy eyebrows. His hair was dark and he had it tied back in a ponytail. He looked like an old hippy."

"How long did you talk?"

"I don't know. Maybe an hour or so."

"What did you talk about?"

"I didn't say much. He talked about clamming. He said they called him the clam whisperer because he always caught more clams than anybody else. He explained how he did it - his technique. And he showed me how to wiggle my toes into the sand just the right way to get at the clams. He called them quahogs."

"Do you remember anything else? Something that could help me find this guy. Did he have a name?"

"He just called himself the clam whisperer."

"I don't think we'll find that in the telephone listing."

"I'm pretty sure he lived nearby. But he had a dog. Aidan, he called him. He didn't like to get his paws wet and he was crippled - wore a contraption, a dog wheelchair."

"Rick, tomorrow you and I are going to go to Narragansett and see if we can find anyone who knows this clam whisperer. We really need someone to alibi you for the time when Morgan was murdered. If we don't find him, it doesn't look good for you. You had motive and opportunity. Your fingerprints will be in the house and you could have easily taken the keys to the car off the hook above the table where you left the check."

"Kara, how did you end up with the check? I left it on the table. Shouldn't you hand it in? It's evidence."

"It places you at the scene so, no, I'm not going to turn it in until I can speak with Lenore Duckworth. And right now, that doesn't seem to be in the stars."

"Thanks, Kara." He stood up and gently handed a sleepy Celia to her mother.

"You need to tell Ruth all of this. She's worried about you, and not telling her will only make things worse."

They listened to the laughter coming from the living room.

"I wanted to protect her. I'll tell her tonight. If I can pry her away from W. C. Fields."

"Promise her I'll lend her the whole boxed set to take home - for as long as she wants."

ož

19

And the poem, I think, is only your voice speaking.
-**Virginia Woolf,** *The Waves*

THE NEXT MORNING EVERYONE was bustling around the house getting ready to start the day. Stewart and Ruth ate a quick breakfast and left early together to get to their classes at the college. Sophia and Gino offered to take Celia on an adventure. The day was now free for Rick and Kara to search for the old hippy and his dog.

"We should start with going to the beach and then to some of the businesses across from The Pier. Hopefully they'll have restored power in that area," Kara said as they climbed into the car.

They spent most of their time speaking with people who were hanging around the seawall watching the surfers. A group of teenagers said they'd seen the old man and his dog, but not lately and no one knew his name. All of the stores in the shopping center were closed. A generator was running as a work crew cleaned up water with a sump pump and tossed saturated sandbags into the back of a pick-up truck. One of the men suggested they go to the pet stores and see if someone could give them a lead. At the Critter Hut in the Wakefield Mall the woman behind the counter said the man and his dog came in to buy a bag of *Alpo* once a month. She didn't expect them back for another week.

"We love Aidan. He's really smart. And the clam whisperer is so proud of him. He says Aidan's the cleverest being he's ever known."

"Did he have an account on file?" Kara asked.

"No, he always pays with cash. He should come in again at the end of the month."

Kara and Rick left the store and sat out in the car deciding where to go next.

"Maybe we should find out where the locals go clamming?"

"I think I know just the person to ask," Kara said taking out her cell phone and dialing the police station. "Leo, is Sergeant Shwinnard around?"

"He's been in and out all morning. He left a few minutes ago. You might be able to track him down in Peace Dale. He had some donations to drop off at the Jonnycake Center."

The sergeant was just driving away from the curb outside the store and heading toward Wakefield as they approached the rotary. A dog hung out the open window on the passenger side and gave them a quizzical look as they chased the car with the horn blaring. Shwinnard pulled into the High Street fire station lot and got out to greet them. Trini jumped into the driver's seat and yipped a few times until Shwinnard introduced him.

"I was supposed to be returning the little guy to his home, but his owner has decided to stay with her daughter a bit longer. There was some flood damage at her place in Matunuck."

"Appears as though he's made himself right at home. Speaking of dogs, have you ever come across a dog with wheels on his hind legs?"

"Sure, the owner is a guy they call the clam whisperer. He walks the dog at The Pier sometimes."

"Do you have any idea where he goes clamming?" Kara asked.

"I can think of a few places, but serious quahoggers around here like to keep their spots secret. You might be able to get some information at the fish store in town, though."

"Thanks for the lead, Sarge."

"I heard you were helping out on the Duckworth case."

Rick looked at Kara who said, "I've helped out a little. Is there any more information on Elliot Scott? Gerry told me you found his cell phone."

"He's still among the missing. Either he's guilty of something and hiding out or he's in trouble. I can't see an actor going days without his phone."

The dog barked. "Looks like Trini thinks I've done enough socializing. Good luck with finding the old guy and his dog."

The manager of the seafood store in town knew Aidan. "He's a great dog! Lots of personality."

"I was wondering if you could tell me where I might find his owner today?"

Kara asked.

"Sometimes he goes down to Potter Pond. But most of the time he he goes to a place off Jerry Brown Farm Road. Hey, Fred." A young man wearing a stained apron came out from room behind the counter. "Fred's dad's a commercial quahogger," he explained.

Fred wiped his hands on the apron. "What can I do for you?"

"They need to find the guy who comes in here with the dog with the wheels"

"Aidan. He's the best."

"We're looking for his owner."

"You mean the clam whisperer." He put air quotes around the words. "My pop told me that guy gets more of a haul with his toes in one hour than any of the five guys working together for him on the boat in a day."

"His pop tends to tell fish tales," the manager informed them.

"Did he mention where he goes clamming?"

Fred looked shocked at the question. "Clammers like to keep their spots secret. If I tell you, I'd have to kill you." He laughed at his own joke.

Rick didn't laugh. "Detective Langley and I need to talk to him in regard to a homicide."

Fred looked at his manager who went to the register and came back with a sheet of paper.

"Draw them a map," he said handing the boy a pencil from the counter.

Kara drove past the spot to and had to turn around. An old, rusty pick-up was parked as far into the bushes as it could go just before the pathway. They followed it and came out to a cove. The dog sat patiently on the edge of the water watching as a man in a bucket hat bobbed up and down throwing shells into a floating basket. He turned when he heard his dog barking and came out of the shallow water.

"Well, hello. Don't I know you?" Rick nodded hopefully. "Wait! Don't tell me, let me think on it a minute. The brain's a little foggy. I know! You're the guy I met on the beach. Rick Car, Rick Carna, Rick Carnaval?"

"Close enough. It's Carnavale," He shook the man's hand.

"This is my friend, Kara Langley. Detective Kara Langley."

"A lady detective! What brings you here to my part of the world?"

"I need your help. Can you remember which night you saw Rick?"

"As a matter of fact, it sticks out in my mind. It was the night of that hit and run. You see, I was friends with Lenore, the woman whose daughter was killed."

"You know Mrs. Duckworth?"

"I was in the Coast Guard with her husband in my younger years. Seems like another lifetime ago. We were stationed at Point Judith. Reggie Duckworth was a good man. We went clamming every Saturday and some weekdays after work. He's the one who gave me my nickname."

Kara never ceased to be amazed at how small the world was. "Do you know what time Rick was with you on the beach?"

"Sure. Aidan wanted to go for a walk after we watched Rachel Maddow. I never miss that program. Like to keep up with what's going on. She knows her stuff."

"So, a little after 10?"

"That would be about right. We went down to the beach. I live in one of those condos that face the water. Takes me three minutes. I had my metal detector, checking the sand to see what I could find when I heard Aidan bark to tell me we weren't alone."

"And how long did you stay on the beach?"

"A couple of hours, I'd say. I got back home just before midnight."

"And Rick was with you all that time?"

"Yup, we walked and I talked. I told him everything he needed to know about clamming. When we got back to the parking lot, he asked me if I needed a ride. He had his taxi. Said he was done for the night and it would be off the meter. I knew he was a nice guy the minute I saw him. Aidan liked him, too and …"

"Mr…" Kara realized she didn't know his name and she hesitated to call him Mr. Whisperer."

"Captain Kurtis Quirk at your service." He gave her a smart salute.

"You've been very helpful, Captain Quirk."

"Please, call me Kurt, Ma'am."

"Kurt, Rick is a person of interest in Morgan Duckworth's death. We'll need you to vouch for him that night. It's really important."

"I don't mind at all. Glad to do a friend a favor. I can go to the station right now, and tell them he was with me."

Rick shook Kurt's hand. "I'd like to go with you." Kara gave Rick a hug and said she would meet him back at the house later. "I have a few things left to do before I meet with Gerry Sullivan. Tell him I'll talk with him later today."

When the gear and the dog's cart had been stowed in the back of the pick-up, Kara waited for them to leave. Aidan sat nestled on the seat between Rick and Kurt.

"If you ever want to learn the best way to get quahogs, I could give you a few pointers," he told Kara. "I don't usually share my tricks with anyone," the clam whisperer said, "but any friend of Rick's is a friend of mine."

"I would like that, Kurt. My dad used to go clamming with my brother down in Galilee. Just off the Point Judith Escape Road. I've always been sorry I never went with them."

"It was nice having company while I worked," he told her and then turned to Rick. "You're not much of a talker, but you're a great listener."

"I call him Chatty Cathy," Kara told him.

Kurt laughed and said, "Everyone needs a nickname even if it's ironic."

ᚥ

20

I shut my eyes and all the world drops dead;
I lift my lids and all is born again.
(I think I made you up inside my head.)

-Sylvia Plath, "Mad Girl's Love Song"

S HE PARKED ALONG THE side of the mill between an antique Harley and an old Volkswagen Beetle with a peace sign painted on the back doors. It brought to mind stories Ruth had shared about her parents who drove around in a painted van back in the 60s.

"According to my parents, I was their love child. They both became architects and some of their designs were cutting edge back in the day. I always feel so stodgy when I go out to visit them in Seattle. They live on a farm and raise llamas. My father tells me I take after his mother. I've seen pictures of her and I'm not so sure it's a compliment."

Kara assured her she was anything but stodgy. "You're the coolest person I know." She was glad she could help her friend because Ruth was always there for everyone else and it was Ruth who had introduced her to Stewart. Kara could never repay her for such a precious gift.

She roamed the halls scanning the artists' names on the outside of the studios and listening to the sounds inside. Behind one closed door, came the pulsing beat of a polka. In another, the whirr of a machine. She glanced into an open room where a weaver worked on her loom to the melodic notes of Eric Satie's *Gymnopeids*.

On the second floor, she found the name she was searching for. She knocked on the double doors. It opened and she called inside, "Selina?"

No answer. She went in, leaving the door ajar, and stood observing the surroundings. A familiar structure set inside a sandbox seemed familiar to her. A castle in the sand. She studied it and then moved on to a worktable where hand bound books covered in embossed leather and assorted feathered quill pens covered its surface. On a small workbench were tools stored in a wooden carpenter's box. A small mallet, files, flat forks and flat tooth chisels. A point chisel and various grades of sandpaper were nearby. On the shelves were materials not yet cut. Alabaster, marble, agate. A lovely mixed-media mask painted gold with twig branches and small birds caught her attention. It reminded her of a Rilke poem she'd once read in college. In Ruth's class.

Artwork hung from the walls behind two screens which gave the feeling one was entering down a path to a beach, sand dunes on either side. On the wall was an oil panting on canvass of ominous black storm clouds hovering above a dark, gray ocean. Underneath the canvass was a blue brocade settee. She sat down to wait. The steamer trunk in front of the couch was unlocked. She opened it and studied the miniatures nestled inside. She heard someone coming down the hallway and they stopped at the door, hesitating before entering. "I'm not opened for sale," she called out to the interloper who was sitting behind the screens on the other end of the room.

Kara stood up and stepped out of the sitting area. "Hello, Selina."

"Oh, it's you. How did you know …?" It suddenly came to her, "Lenore."

"Yes. She said you came here to work. Do you give lessons?"

"No, I use the studio to do consignments. I don't usually have people walk in off…." She moved toward the table. "Are you here to see about lessons? There is another sculptor who has a studio outside of the mill, in the back. She's an excellent teacher. I could bring you there now and introduce you if you'd like." She moved quickly toward the door, hoping Kara would follow.

"I'm actually here to ask you a few questions."

"I was just getting ready to leave. I only came to give my rent to Lynn."

"I won't be long."

"What do you want to know?"

"I was hoping you could tell me where I could find your ex husband."

"Elliot? I would imagine he's in New York. I can give you his phone number."

"I've called but there's no answer."

"You should send a text. He answers his texts."

"When was the last time you saw Elliot?"

Selina hesitated before saying, "We went out to lunch at the Oyster House in Matunuck last Friday. He was going to catch the train back to the city. I gave him a ride to the station in Kingston."

"He told his fiancée he would be back on Saturday."

Kara noticed that Selina flinched at the word fiancée.

"He must have intended to stay the night. Do you have any idea where he would have stayed?"

"He likes the Blueberry Cove Inn in Narragansett."

"The police have contacted all of the hotels and B & B's."

"Then maybe he's back at his apartment in New York and he's just not answering his phone."

"He lives with Sunny, his fiancée." Again Kara noticed a reaction. "Sunny's the one who reported him missing."

Selina had moved away distancing herself from Kara. She switched off the lamp which was casting a light on the castle, shining through the alabaster, causing it to be transparent.

"Where are you staying?"

"I have a cottage at Moonstone."

"They evacuated everyone from that area this weekend. Each house was checked."

"I've been spending time here in my studio. I sometimes fall asleep. Lynn can tell you, she woke me up on Saturday morning."

"Have you returned to the house since then?"

"Why are you asking me all these questions? I have no idea where Elliot is. He probably just didn't want to go back to his girlfriend. I'm sure he has other friends in New York. I told you, I dropped him off at the train."

Kara moved to stand closer to Selina. She could see the tenseness in the woman's neck. "Selina, if you'd like to talk to me, I'll listen." She pressed a business card into her hand. The skin was smooth, like marble, and ice cold.

"I've told you what I know."

"The police would like to speak with you again. Detective Gerry Sullivan is in charge of the investigation."

"I've spoken to him. He has my number."

"It seems your phone is not on. He hasn't been able to contact you. I would go to the station as soon as possible and tell him what you've told me about taking Elliot to Kingston on Friday."

Kara left her standing in the doorway. A few minutes went by until Selina came outside and went to the back lot to get her car. As she drove away from the mill, Kara hoped she was heading for the police station.

Kara called Gerry Sullivan from her car and asked to meet with him and his team to give them information she'd been gathering.

"Rick Carnavale came by this morning. He said you'd helped him track down the guy he was with the night of the accident. To tell you the truth, we thought he was trying to send us on a wild goose chase with his clam whisperer story. I got a statement from them both."

"I spoke with Selina Borelli and told her you wanted to meet with her. I think you need to obtain search warrants for her studio at Shady Lea in North Kingstown and the house at Moonstone. It may lead us to information on where to find Elliot Scott. I'll be at the station in twenty minutes. Hopefully, Selina will be there."

ℜ

It didn't surprise her that Selina was not at the police station. Gerry and Kara set off in separate cars toward Matunuck. Road crews were still working on power lines and trucks were pushing back the sand that had blown on to the road.

No one was home at Selina's place. The back door was unlocked. They entered and called out her name. Although the water had crept up to the deck, it didn't appear to have seeped inside the building.

"Selina's not here. Any other ideas where she might be?" When she didn't answer, he went into the bedroom and found Kara crouched down, looking under the bed. "Are you searching for anything in particular?"

"I'm not sure, but I've got a hunch."

On the floor of the closet, underneath a man's *Burberry* raincoat, she found what she was looking for. She took a picture of the pair of shoes. Her phone rang. It was Sophia. She'd received a call from the hospital that Lenore had regained consciousness and wanted to see Kara.

"Gerry, these need to be bagged and brought directly to the forensics lab. Give them to Professor Hill. I have a few more things left to do, but tell him I'll talk to him later."

☙

Lenore was sleeping and the nurse had placed a chair by the side of the bed for Kara. She didn't awaken until darkness had settled into the room. She smiled when Kara stood up to show her that she was wearing the blue sweater. The nurse came in to tend to her and Kara went outside to call home. Ruth answered and assured her everything was fine. Rick had arrived home and told her the news. She promised to save some dinner for her. She could hear her friends in the background laughing.

"Kara, thank you."

"You're welcome, Ruth. Tell Stewart and the others I'm almost done. I'll be home soon." She turned the phone to record and placed it on the stand by the bed then took Lenore's hand in her own.

"Marie and Pierre?" the woman tried to raise her head but could not move it from the pillow.

"The Curies are doing fine. Pat has them with her. She's the one who found you and called the rescue."

Lenore touched the sleeve of the sweater. "The check?"

"I still have it. I guessed you might have placed it somewhere. It's your writing. You sent the checks to Rick, didn't you?"

"Yes. I didn't know he'd be so angry." She asked for a sip of water and closed her eyes for a moment. "He drove me to the house in the morning. I didn't expect Morgan to be home. She had tickets to a play. He returned at night. She came to the door. He got out of the car and handed her the check. She began yelling at him, but he didn't stop to listen. He just left."

"Do you know what time that was?"

"Around 9:30. We'd had an argument earlier in the day. I wanted to take the Spider. The caddy wasn't working. The keys were hanging on the hook and she said, 'Over my dead body.' I went up to my room to get some fall clothes I'd left in the closet. I heard the car start up and looked out to see it going down the driveway. I thought Morgan had taken it."

"The keys were on the hook when you went up to your room?"

"Yes."

"You need to rest. I've taped your statement and I'll give it to the police. I'll be back tomorrow."

"My daughter hated me."

"Lenore, you did your best for Morgan."

"She hated me. The candy. It had pills in it. I'm sure. I didn't take enough myself to put me in the hospital."

"You think Morgan drugged the candy? Why would she do that?"

"Money. She was afraid I would change my will. Check the candy from the box she'd left upstairs. I brought it downstairs to eat because I'd given away all of mine as gifts at the luncheon."

"I'll get them to the lab right away."

"I took my pills and had some wine that night. Too much wine. I noticed the bottom of some of the pieces of chocolate were sticky. Morgan liked to open the chocolates a little to see what was inside before she ate them. I didn't think anything of it."

"You'll need the house key. It's in my jacket pocket."

"I have it. I went there today. Selina came by. I told her you were in the hospital. Does she have a key to your house?"

"No, but there may still be one hidden under the sun dial. Over near the laurel bushes. Strange. I had a dream about Selina the night Morgan died. I looked out the window of the nursery and she was at the hedge making topiaries. It seemed so real." She closed her eyes.

"Lenore, you get some sleep."

"Do you know what the irony is? She wasted a completely good box of expensive chocolates. I'd already changed my will."

And Kara thought about the real irony. Morgan had died before she would find out there was nothing left for her to inherit when her mother died. Someone had made sure of that. The suspect list had narrowed, and Kara knew the clues were falling in place. She just needed to discover where Elliot Scott was hiding out and all of the puzzle pieces would be on the board ready to fit together.

Her next call was to Gerry. ""I spoke with Lenore. You need to send a team over to her house on Ocean Road. I'll drop off the key on my way home. Have them bring kits to gather up the medication from the bathroom cabinet on the third floor and the wine glass and the box of chocolates in the study to take to Professor Hill at the forensics lab. And there's a piece of cake in the microwave on the kitchen shelf. Have them bag that too." She put her hand into her sweater pocket but decided not to mention the check. She had some questions that needed to be answered. "I'll see you tomorrow morning. Plan on going on a field trip."

cs

21

I have you fast in my fortress,
And will not let you depart,
But put you down into the dungeon
In the round-tower of my heart.
And there will I keep you forever,
Yes, forever and a day,
Till the walls shall crumble to ruin,
And Moulder in dust away!

-Henry Wadsworth Longfellow, "The Children's Hour"

A S SOON AS SHE knew Professor Hill was in the lab, she called to
let him know what had been happening. "I'm planning on coming
to work this afternoon. I expect you'll find diazepam or zolpidem in the
candy. I told Gerry to make sure the team bagged the pills from Lenore's
medicine cabinet and brought them in along with the wine glass, the
cake, and the chocolates."

"I was in at the crack of dawn and did the trace on those shoes. You can
look at the report when you get here," he said. "I spoke with the captain
and they're preparing an arrest warrant. Any idea where Elliot Scott is?"

"I have a hunch. I'll see you this afternoon."

Stewart came out to the kitchen with Celia.

"Guess who just woke up? And she wants to know where everybody's
disappeared to."

"It was fun having a full house. But I like getting back to normal."

Together they prepared breakfast and made plans for the rest of the day.

"I'm going to take Celia to work with me. I've had to share her lately and today is going to be our day. I've got some papers to correct and a few student meetings. And we can do lunch at the faculty center. She'll be a big hit."

"Sounds like a wonderful day. I appreciate you're stepping in so I can finish up this case."

"You think you have it all figured out?"

"I just have one or two things to do and, yes, I think it will be solved."

"Celia, your momma is a smart cookie. Nothing gets past her." He took her little hands and helped her to clap. Kara bowed and gave her a kiss.

"Thank you both for that resounding vote of confidence."

℃

"So, where are you taking me?" Gerry asked.

"I thought you might appreciate a bit of culture," Kara said.

"My wife is always getting on me about going to a play or a concert. I tend to like spending my free time on the couch with some nachos and cheese and watching the Patriots in the comfort of my own man cave. Go Pats!"

"Well, your wife will be happy to know you are going to spend some of your time today experiencing art."

"Art? Like in paintings and statues?"

"Exactly."

"Are you taking me up to RISD? Cuz I'm not really into museums. When I retire, I'm definitely not becoming a museum guard. I'd go crazy standing around all day surrounded by all that silence. I'd make a better mall cop."

"We're not going to Providence. We have art right here in our own backyard." Kara pointed at a sign. "Shady Lea Historic District, slow down and get ready to turn right on Shady Lea Road."

They arrived at the mill and he parked in the rear. "Look at this place. I never knew it was back here."

"Wait until you see the inside. It's an artists' colony. We have some time to walk around until the custodian arrives. Lynn gave me his number to call when we got here."

They strolled the halls, looking into the studios that were open as artists worked. From some of the rooms, the sound of tools mixed with music could be heard.

"This place is awesome. The old wood plank floors, the high ceilings and those beams. The gigantic windows. It's like a living museum."

They'd reached the second-floor studio and she knocked on the double doors. "Selina?" There was no answer.

Gerry looked at the nameplate on the wall. "Selina Borelli. Do you think she's been hiding out? She hasn't answered her phone since last week."

"She was here yesterday paying her rent. I had called Lynn and she said Selina usually comes in later in the afternoon, so I thought I'd find her. I told her you wanted to talk with her."

The custodian arrived and Gerry showed him his police ID. He unlocked the doors and let them into the studio and excused himself. He had some work to do.

"I'll come back to lock up after you leave. If you need to get in again, here's my cell." He handed it to Gerry.

The room was already bright with sunbeams streaming in but Kara immediately went to the light and switched it on. Gerry was mesmerized by the sculpture and the fact that he could see through all the walls and into the turrets. Kara showed him a photo she'd taken of a house with a fountain in front.

"It looks just like this castle."

"I took it when I was at Lenore's yesterday. It's the property next door. Look closely."

He knelt down and studied the structure.

"What do you see?"

"It looks like there's someone in each of the towers."

"Exactly."

"A man in one, a woman in the other."

"I would agree." She waited.

"Do you think Elliot Scott is in the house next door to the Duckworth estate?"

"I do."

"Do you have proof?"

"There was a car parked outside when Selina was at the Duckworth house with me, but it wasn't there when I went over to see if anyone was home. I saw her drive the same car out of the parking lot here at the mill yesterday. And we know she didn't go to the station to see you or return to her cottage. And she mentioned to me in passing that she hadn't heard the dogs barking at Lenore's in the morning. I called to find out who owns the property and got in touch with him yesterday. Preston Lightsey says Selina is house sitting for him. She was there the night that Morgan was murdered. Lenore saw her coming through the laurel hedge."

"What made you connect the house to her?"

"The fountain in front of the house has a sculpture in it. Lightsey bought one of Selina's works. Two lovers embracing with a third person watching. *La Trahison. The Betrayal*. I believe Elliot Scott is inside that house. I gave the owner's contact information to your captain this morning and advised him to get a warrant to search the place."

"And there's something else you need to see." She opened the trunk and took out the maquette, placing it on the coffee table. It was a miniature re-creation of the area around *Druidsdream*. The altar, the columns, the Druid's chair, the cemetery, and a body in a gray running outfit, lying by the side of the road with a small metal sports car pinning her legs to the ground. "I have a warrant for you to take this in as evidence. There are journals on the table by the window. You should take those, too."

"Do you think she's with Scott?"

"I believe she went to him yesterday. I'm not sure if he's involved. He may just be an innocent victim. She's not well."

"Do you mean she's physically ill?"

"Physically and mentally. I think the cancer has returned. She looks very frail. And I did some checking. She spent time in an institution after her marriage collapsed. The medicine she was prescribed is for schizophrenia. She hasn't been taking it."

"We have enough to arrest her for Morgan's murder. Now we just have to bring her in."

☙

Elliot Scott was under observation at South County Hospital. They'd found him locked in a room just below one of the turrets. He told the police he'd been drugged and left to die.

"I put a police guard on his hospital room," Gerry told Kara when he phoned later in the day. "If he's in danger from Selina, as he says, he'll be safe. If he was helping her, then he's not going anywhere. They're doing a tox screen on him now."

"Selina wasn't in the house?"

"No. The custodian called and said he thought he'd seen her at the mill. She was all bundled up with a scarf around her face so he couldn't be sure. We sent someone there and we have police watching the studio and the cottage. We found prescriptions for pills. *Lumateperone*. We sent someone to find out if she's shown up at the psychiatrist's office. I don't know where else she could be. She has no friends."

"I'm at the forensics lab with Professor Hill. I'm checking the paperwork to make sure it's all in order. Call me right away if you find her."

"I think we've got it all covered," Hill said. "The glass shards imbedded in the bottom of the cork sandals were a match to the car's broken headlight. That should seal it up. Good job, Sherlock." He handed them to her.

"*Mephisto Lissandra* Sandals. Sophia found a pair just like these in Morgan's closet. Very expensive. My friend has a type of radar for expensive clothes. I looked at the soles and it brought to mind the piece of cork we examined in the lab."

"From under the accelerator pedal in the Spider." He nodded.

"I was just glancing over the results from the chocolates they brought in from Lenore's."

"Traces of *diazepam*," he confirmed. "But the residue from the wine glass was *lumateperone*. That's the medication for Selina's schizophrenia. It's not either of the two drugs they brought in from Lenore Duckworth's medicine cabinet."

"Yes. It's Selina's. She probably put it into the wine bottle that day when they had lunch."

"And Lenore was already on *zolpidem* for her insomnia. It's a wonder the mix of drugs and liquor didn't kill the woman."

"I think I'll go by the hospital and see how she is. Do you need me to do anything else for you?"

"All set. I'll get the report to Gerry Sullivan today. I hope they find her soon. She doesn't seem to be very stable."

"She didn't use her last three prescriptions. The ones we found in her house. If she's not taking her medication, she definitely could be a danger."

"I know that look, Kara. You've done enough on this case. Let the cops bring her in."

She chuckled as she patted him on the back. "I'll see you tomorrow, Dennis."

"Once a cop, always a cop," she heard him mutter as she left the lab.

At the hospital, they told her Lenore had been sleeping most of the day. Kara looked in on her but decided not to wake her up. Instead, she returned to the estate and found the key under the sundial.

She let herself in and walked around the rooms taking in the expensive artwork adorning the walls and the well-polished antiques. She went upstairs to the nursery and opened the doors to the balcony. She imagined what it must have been like the day Angela had died. Lenore lost two children that day. To lose a child. It was unimaginable. She closed the doors and came inside.

On the night table by Lenore's bed she found the journal. Selina had returned one last time. Kara thought of Silas, the hired man, and of Mary's words to Warren. "Home is the place where, when you have to go there, They have to take you in." She sat in the rocking chair and read through the pages until she came to the last entry.

She knows. Her dark eyes saw right through me. The hope chest wasn't locked. All hope gone. I'm sure it wasn't the work of ghosts. A human hand turned the key to look at the maquettes. I would have liked to finish the last of them. The blood - not done. No matter. The altar, the columns, the graves, the Druid's chair remain in place, all carved from the same quarry stone. I think

Joseph would be pleased. The light is shining inside my castle. A going away gift. I've decided to go away. Nothing left but to go away. Betrayed. Nothing much to leave behind. When she touched my hand, she knew. I could feel it as her fingers brushed across my skin. My body was like alabaster and she could see inside to the depths of my broken soul. She tapped the metal against my surface and could hear the ringing. And she realized I wasn't sorry for what I'd done. I'm not sorry. Morgan was a terrible person. She deserved to die. I would do it again.

Kara closed the book and put it into the pocket of her sweater, then called Stewart. "I'll be home soon. Give Celia a kiss for me."

಩

The Aftermath

We may sink and settle on the waves.
The sea will drum in my ears.
The white petals will be darkened with seawater.
They will float for a moment and then sink.
Rolling over, the waves will shoulder me under.
Everything falls in a tremendous shower, dissolving me.

-Virginia Woolf, *The Waves*

22

When anxious, uneasy and
bad thoughts come, I go
to the sea, and the sea
drowns them out with its
great wide sounds,
cleanses me with its noise,
and imposes a
rhythm upon everything
in me that is bewildered
and confused.

-**Rainer Maria Rilke**, *The Selected Poetry of Ranier Maria Rilke*

THE SAND WAS ICY cold on her bare feet, but the pond still held some of the warmth of the summer. She dipped the toy bucket into the water and brought it back to the castle she'd been working on for hours in the early morning darkness. She'd searched for the remnants of the castle she'd made at the end of the summer, before it had all gone so wrong. Nothing from that creation had survived. Not even the bottles. The hurricane had been brutal and unforgiving to the beach. More of it had eroded. Disappeared. Soon nothing would be left except the ocean itself.

When the turret was completed, she took the last journal from her bag. There'd been many more before. This had only one entry. A quote by Rilke. She placed the leather-bound book in the middle for protection against the tide. Perhaps someone would discover it before the next rains melted the ink into the pages. Bled the words together so they made no sense to anyone but the writer. She collected the larger stones, going into the dunes in spite of the no trespassing signs. The plovers would forgive her this and she made sure to step lightly. She worried the rocks would tear the wool, but the material held strong. Selina walked toward the waves, stopping only for a second to pick up a sea star and place it in her pocket with the rocks. It had lost one of its arms in battle. She thought it might be nice to lie on the beach watching it regenerate but there weren't enough hours left in her lifetime. Starfish were the ultimate survivors. She would carry it back to the sea with her on her journey.

She didn't feel the cold as she moved forward. A wave splashed her face, its salt stung her eyes. In her mind she remembered Rilke's words, the ones she'd written in the journal. "You are not a drop in the ocean. You are the entire ocean in a drop."

The stones dragged her down until she could no longer see the sky. Just the ocean covering her, washing her sins. A hiding place from the pain. A shelter from the storm. She was going home at last.

ßà

23

The price of love is not so high
As never to have loved once in the dark
Beyond foreseeing. Now, as dawn gleams pale,
Upon small wind-fanned waves, amid white sails

-Michael R. Burch, "To Have Loved"

ARRANGEMENTS HAD BEEN MADE for Lenore to leave the hospital at the end of October. She'd hired nurses to care for her and informed her friends at Sea View she was moving back home. Pat Nailor and the Curies were there to welcome her and get her settled in. Kara and Sophia stopped by for a short visit and brought Celia with them. Lenore sat holding the baby. Much to Celia's delight, the dogs raced around the room wagging their tales. They were happy to be home. They had tea at the dining room table and then the nurse announced sternly that it was time for her patient to take a nap. She insisted on going out to the porch and stood waving at them and blowing kisses to Celia. Back inside, she wrote a few short notes, then went to bed. The nurse pulled the drapes, shutting out the sunlight. Lenore Duckworth never woke up. She'd known in her heart that she'd come home to die.

ଔ

Elliot Scott returned to New York and was getting ready for a new part off Broadway. One morning in October, a gift arrived at their apartment. A large crate. Sunny couldn't imagine what it could be. Elliot knew what was inside, and he carefully unwrapped the alabaster sculpture from its mounds of packing peanuts. They placed it in the living room along with their other wedding gifts. Elliot read the note and put it in his pocket. "Enjoy your fairytale. Selina"

CZ

It had taken two weeks for her body to wash to shore. Lenore had made all of the arrangements while they were still searching. It would be a simple service. People were notified of the place and time when her ashes would be spread on the sands and taken back out to sea.

Selina had murdered Morgan. She'd been staying at the Lightsey estate next door and had come through the hedge that night to visit Lenore. She hadn't expected to see Morgan leaving the house. She took the key to the car from the hook above the hall table and had driven the Spider to wait for Morgan to come to the Druid's Circle. She knew her old friend's habits. She'd been keeping watch on her. Afterwards, Selina returned the car to the garage, placed the key back on the hook, and disappeared into the darkness of the house next door. It was all in her last journal. The case could finally be closed, and Selina could be put to her final rest.

CZ

Rick was raking leaves in his front yard when the postman came up the walk and stopped to give him a certified letter. It was from Lenore's lawyer and informed him he was the beneficiary of her estate and gave him a date and time to appear for a reading of the will. Also included was a note.

> *Richard, I can't give you back the life you had taken away and this is not meant to make up for that loss. I'm sorry for all the pain you've been through. I loved Evie, too. And my heart broke when she died. But you have a new life now and I want you to enjoy every moment you've both been given. Love, Lenore.*

Ruth appeared from around the back of the house with a shovel. "Hey, I think I'm going to need some help planting these blueberry bushes."

To her surprise, he took her in his arms. "I think we can both manage that. But before we start digging, I have something to share with you."

☙

Stewart came into the house and announced, "Celia, you've got mail!"

Kara stopped feeding her and wiped her chin with her bib. "Your very first letter. Aunt Sophia will be pleased. She'll have to add a separate section for correspondence in your Baby Langley loose-leaf binder."

"It's from Connor and Billy. You're invited to a Halloween Party at their house next week. We'll have to add this to your social calendar. Why don't I just finish feeding you while Momma calls Auntie Sophia so she can make you your first Halloween costume? We know she'd never let you go out in public in those cute kitty pajamas I bought you."

They exchanged seats.

"Okay, here comes the rocket. Bzzzzzz," He swirled the spoon around and put the pureed squash on her lips. "Okay, open up. Mmmmm. Delicious." He tried to coax her to eat more. "Yummy squash. Mmmmm.

"Muhmuhmuhmuhm," the baby answered.

"Kara, did you hear what Celia just said? Say it again, Celia."

"Mmmmuhmuhmuh."

"Momma! She said her first word, Kara. Momma! Something else for the book."

Kara laughed at the two of them as Stewart tried to get his daughter to eat and the food dribbled from her mouth. *At least it isn't blue. Orange is definitely the color for the fall. I can live with that.*

☙

EPILOGUE

Lifting my head
I watch the bright moon,
Lowering my head
I dream that I'm home.

-**Li Po,** "Quiet Night Thoughts"

Sophia always sewed her own Halloween costume and tried to convince the group to let her design theirs. Ruth and Rick usually gave in to her but this year they wouldn't be spending All Hallows Eve with their friends. Ruth had a conference in Boston, and they'd decided to enjoy a getaway alone together. Sophia turned her attention to Kara and Stewart.

"You'd make spectacular Ike and Tina Turners!" she declared.

Kara informed her she and Stewart already had their costumes.

"But I've got a wig and a sexy dress you'd look great in, Kara. And Gino could borrow an electric guitar for Stewart from one of the musicians at the Courthouse Center for the Arts."

"Sophia, I don't think I could live with Stewart doing an Ike Turner impression. He'd be chasing me around singing 'Rollin, rollin, rollin on the river'. 'Proud Mary' is not one of my favorite dance tunes. Promise me you won't even suggest it to him. You can make Celia's outfit, this year." Then she added, "As long as it's not Baby Yoda."

ॐ

Two days later, Sophia had finished the costume. "I decided to be authentic. Basil Rathbone rather than the Benedict Cumberbatch Sherlock," she explained to Kara later when she was fitting Celia for her costume. Although I do love the way they dress Cumberbatch – the long wool guard's coat with the blue wool scarf. Tres Chic. A bit too much for a baby."

"And you don't think this is a bit too much?" Kara asked, knowing full well her answer.

"I suppose you would have dressed her as a pumpkin?"

"I was thinking more along the lines of a cute, little black cat."

"You can dress Stewart up as a cute, little black cat, but as long as I have a sewing machine, my niece is never going to be dressed up as a cliché. And what has Stewart, our friendly neighborhood astrophysicist, chosen for a costume this year? And please don't tell me he's going as Neil Degrasse Tyson again."

"No. This year he's decided to go as a nerdy science teacher. He has those eyeglasses he duct taped together and he borrowed a lab coat from school and a beaker. And he's wearing that bowtie I gave him for his birthday."

"So, he's going to the party dressed as himself? The nutty professor. Very original! Maybe I'll go as a nurse!" She whispered something in Celia's ear. Kara heard the word *plebeian*. Her daughter was going to have a fantastic vocabulary when she started to say real words. Sophia broke into her thoughts. "What about you? What is your winning costume going to be?"

"I was thinking Columbo. To go along with the detective theme you're setting."

"So you've dug out one of Stewart's old raincoats, took a pad and pencil from the desk, and picked up a chewed-up cigar from the sidewalk?"

"I was hoping Gino would have an old chewed up cigar somewhere."

"You are a tall, attractive, black woman. How do you intend to pull off a short, pasty-faced, middle-aged man look? The only way that costume will win you anything is if you find yourself a live Bassett Hound and name it Dog."

"I don't really care about winning anything."

"Then you certainly won't be disappointed," Sophia said.

◌ဩ

Carl Sullivan called for a show of hands to vote for the best costume. "It's unanimous. Celia Langley as baby Sherlock Holmes!" he called out.

Connor danced around and applauded with glee

Stewart held up the winner in the costume Sophia had made for her. A tiny Inverness coat, Deerstalker hat, and briar pipe. They took a picture to give to Professor Hill to put on the bulletin board at the lab. "He'll love it!" Carl said.

Gino and Sophia, aka Sonny and Cher, got the prize for Best Dressed Couple. And, to Stewart's delight, he was awarded Most Authentic Costume.

"Look, we both got gift certificates to the movies! We can double date." Stewart proudly showed off his prize to Sophia who just shook her head and avoided looking at Kara.

Jess announced that food was being served and everyone headed for the pot-luck seafood buffet set up in the dining room. Clam cakes, stuffies, calamari, steamers and a big pot of chowder filled the table.

Gerry brought a plate of food over and sat next to Kara. He was dressed as Columbo, too and had a stuffed basset hound in his raincoat pocket. "We could be twins. Where's your Dog?"

She laughed. "I was originally thinking Dog would be a good outfit for Celia, but her aunt had other ideas. And I've learned not to argue with Sophia."

"I wanted to thank you again for all of the help you gave us. We'd still be digging up clues. Carl was right - you've got great instincts."

"Thanks, Gerry, but your team did most of the footwork and interviews and paperwork. I never really liked that part of the job. And frankly, I find it sad. People always get hurt and there's no way to fix it for them."

"But if we do the job right, we can see that justice is done and the guilty ones are held to account. That the victims are avenged."

"There is that. But I feel I'm contributing with my work at the forensics lab and I like the flexibility I have being able to consult. My mom died when I was a kid. I want to spend as much time with Celia and Stewart as I can."

Carl announced they would be heading out for the celebration on the beach in fifteen minutes. People began to clean up and grab cups of hot coffee to take with them. Connor asked Kara if he could ride with them in the car next to Celia and she wasn't sure who was happier, Billy or him, when she said yes.

ଓ

The night was crisp and a wind was blowing in from the ocean. People were bundled up and some were circling around admiring the bonfire as the flames shot up into the night sky. The moon was a tiny sliver, but there were hundreds of stars above their heads. It seemed like everyone from town was huddled on blankets spread out along the beach. Rick waved to Kurt and he joined their little group standing close by the fire trying to stay warm.

Aidan sat quietly watching as the two labra doodles zigzagged around the revelers on the beach and ran in and out of the waves. A woman called out, "Marie, Pierre, come out of the water, now!" He remembered what it was like to be a pup. Not a care in the world. He was cute and smart and the world was his oyster, as Kurt often told him. Not being a dog who liked oysters, or any other creature living in a shell or coming out of the ocean, for that matter, he was never sure of what those words meant. But the way Kurt said it made him think it must be a good thing. Kurt said and did a lot of things that made no sense to him. *Who in their right mind whispers to clams?* He'd seen his share of clams and was pretty sure they didn't have ears. He prided himself on being an extremely sensible dog, or so people often remarked in his presence. But Kurt was his best friend - the best friend anyone could ever have.

Aidan sometimes had dreams that Kurt was a farmer and they spent their days in a nice warm barn where he never had to get his paws wet. And they were surrounded by sweet, friendly, chubby animals. Sheep, and goats, and cows, and pigs, and chickens. He closed his eyes.

Ahhhhhhhhh meat!

Marie and Pierre, followed close behind by two little boys, ran up the beach toward him. The dogs stopped for a moment to shake their fur enthusiastically next to a group of people cradling cups with steam rising from the tops. Aidan loved the smell of hot coffee.

"Ay! Whatsamattawitchoose?" One of the men yelled at them. They paid no attention to him and ran back into the ocean.

A pretty lady with long, silky black hair, pulled on his arm. "Gino they're only puppies. I think they'd make marvelous pets for Celia, don't you? I heard they need a new home."

The older boy wrestled the naked one to the ground and another dog pounced on top of them thinking it was a game. "Max get off me!" He was trying to pull a tee shirt over the younger child's head and a man came to help. "It's cold, and he's running around with no clothes. Do something, Dad. It's like he's being raised by wolves!"

A sensible boy. Aidan thought they would get along well.

The father stretched his neck up and howled at the moon. The puppies joined in and then everyone was howling.

Ahhhhhhhhh, youth!

He felt a chill and moved in closer to the bonfire. A man stooped over him and opened his jacket, trying to coax a tiny, rat-like creature to come out. "Look, Trini. Look at this nice doggy. Don't you want to come out and play?" Trini made it clear he wanted no part of another dog or of the festivities. The man zippered his jacket and gave Aidan a bone. He put out a paw to shake his hand. "Now that is a dog with class. Did you see that Trini?" But Trini was hunkered down and it was apparent to Aidan he had no intention of sticking his tiny bald head out to learn some manners.

Kurt bent down and asked how he was doing. Aidan looked into his eyes. "You're tired, old boy. It's time for us to go home."

Home. He loved hearing that word even more than *dinner*. No matter what he was doing, he always came running when Kurt would call out, "Come get your dinner, Aidan."

They left the beach just as the music started and everyone began to sing and dance. "It's a marvelous night for a moon dance neath the cover of October skies ...." Aidan turned to listen and then lifted his nose toward the sky.

"AAAAAHHHHOOOOOOOOOOOOH!"

"What are you doing, buddy? Time to go home."

He hurried to catch up to his friend, who gave him a pat on the head. "Good boy. Let's get you home."

Ahhhhhhhhhh home.

Photos & History

The "Beach" Book

Last Castle in the Sand is the beach book that fans of the South County Mysteries have wanted me to write. Unlike the other books in the series, this does not center around one village. Rather it travels along the coastline to bring in some of the many historic places that make up this part of Southern Rhode Island, the Ocean State.

Narragansett

Casino from The Rockingham Looking South

Rhode Island's miles of coastal beaches have always been popular vacation spots where people escape to the breezes of its sandy shoreline, away from the heat of the summer months. Narragansett morphed from a sleepy village to a favorite resort destination when visitors began arriving by steamboat in 1848. In 1876, with its direct rail connections, people from cities like New York and Boston hopped aboard the Narragansett Pier Railroad to stay at the hotels, which had sprung up along the oceanfront. These grand hotels became quite popular with rich businessmen and their families from New York, New Jersey, and Philadelphia. In 1884, the Casino was the center for the fashionable crowds to gather. In 1877, those rich businessmen began erecting grand homes and by 1899, the allure for these socialites had diminished. Some of their mansions still stand today although the oceanfront is no longer lined by grand hotels. A fire at the Rockingham Hotel in September of 1900 destroyed the Casino, sparing the Towers, but other buildings around the Pier, were not so fortunate. Today, this area is now Veteran's Memorial Park. In the years to follow, fires, hurricanes, and urban renewal saw the decline of the grand Victorian hotels that were once the heart of this beach resort during Narragansett's Golden Era. Today, during the summer, the beaches are filled with locals and people traveling down for a day out with friends and family.

This is the neighborhood where Dr. Morgan Duckworth takes her last run under the Towers, around the monument, and toward the Witches' Altar.

Gladstone Hotel & Grounds, Narragansett

*Joseph Peace Hazard was
the son of Rowland and
Mary Peace Hazard.*

Hazard Castle Home of Joseph Peace Hazard

Dunmere, residence of R. G. Dun of New York

Narragansett Pier, circa 1898

The Rockingham

Casino, Beach looking North, Rockingham

Along the Matunuck Water Front

Matunuck

The name Matunuck is taken from the Native American word meaning "lookout" and is where the Narragansett Indian Tribe once made its summer encampment. In the early 20th Century, it became a popular summer destination for out-of-towners. The locals who grew up in this village continue to share cherished memories of a much quieter lifestyle. Matunuck and Moonstone Beaches were the playgrounds where they swam, went clamming, crabbed, and rode horseback along the shore. There is a palpable nostalgia as they speak of the times spent together when this was once their small community of family and friends.

Two of the historic places from the book are the Carpenter-Perry Grist Mill, still in operation, and Theatre-By-the-Sea, which continues to offer plays during the summer season. And through the character of Rolly, I include memories from one of the most notable events for those living on the coast, the devastating 1938 Hurricane, which swept away many homes in this seaside village.

SCENES FROM 1938 HURRICANE

Theatre-by-the-Sea in Matunuck

The Carpenter-Perry Grist Mill

Pictures of the Carpenter-Perry Grist Mill

The Mill at Shady Lea

The Mill at Shady Lea

A short drive from Narragansett, along Route 1, is the historic Shady Lea District with its artisans' community housed in the mill along the Mattatuxet River in North Kingstown. Known in 1820 as the Springdale Factory, it is one of the surviving textile mills that once made woolen blankets for the soldiers during the Civil War.

The current owner, Lynn Krim, spent time with me sharing her memories of King Fastener, the metal staple business her father, Ambrose Reisert, ran from the mill for 30 years. As a teenager in the summers, she worked alongside the women and children. Reisert, in the 1990s, began the mill's transformation into the artists' haven now home to 40 studios and the creative souls who share their work with the public. Lynn describes the mill as a place of bonding where artists work together and support one another. During my conversations with her, she shared the stories about ghosts that still roam the building where the sculptor Selina has her studio in *Last Castle in the Sand.*

The King Fastener work force

Acknowledgments

Sincere thanks to my team: Michael Grossman, publisher; Dr. Joyce Stevos, editor; and Zach Perry, cover and map designer. To those who helped with the research and photos, I send a special shoutout: Thomas Frawley, the North Kingstown Free Library; Sam Judd, the Maury Loontjens Memorial Library in Narragansett; Lynn Krim, owner of The Mill at Shady Lea; Elizabeth Lind, Shady Lea artisan; John Lacroix and all of those who grew up in Matunuck and continue to share the love of the area on their local Facebook page; and to Sean McCarron for sharing memories of his buddy Aidan with me.

Although Charley, my cherished partner and Muse, was by my side, encouraging, supporting, and advising me throughout the writing of all of my children's books and the South County mysteries, he will not be there for the launching of *Last Castle in the Sand*. He died, suddenly, in March and with him, the joy we shared in creating these amazing worlds together, was suddenly taken from my life.

Michael, Joyce, and Zach have assisted me in putting the finishing touches on *Last Castle* and it will be published, as Charley would have wished, this fall.

To all of the awesome fans of the South County Mystery Series, I send my sincere gratitude for your continuing enthusiasm and loyalty with hope the South County "beach" book everyone has looked forward to will prove to be well worth the wait.

ABOUT THE AUTHOR

Claremary Sweeney is a writer/photographer from South Kingstown, Rhode Island. She spent her earlier years in the field of education and now, retired, she uses her imagination to create stories that can be enjoyed by children of all ages and the young at heart.

Within her first book, *A Berkshire Tale*, are the original ten ZuZu Stories about the adventures of a kitten born on a farm in the Berkshire Hills. It's filled with the settings that make this area an historic as well as a cultural center in western Massachusetts.

Written in verse, *Carnivore Conundrum* concerns Adonis, a little pitcher plant. He decides one morning, after a traumatic incident with a fly flailing around in his digestive juices, that he will be swearing off meat. His mother and all the plants and creatures in the garden must find a way to coax this stubborn baby to eat again.

Last Castle in the Sand is the fifth addition to Sweeney's South County Mystery Series. As in the previous four books, it incorporates local history and settings with familiar coastal scenes from Matunuck, Moonstone,and Narragansett that have long enticed visitors to the shores of our Ocean State. *Last Train to Kingston* first introduced South Kingstown Detective

Kara Langley and her friends. This was soon followed by *Last Rose on the Vine*, *Last Carol of the Season*, and *Last Sermon for a Sinner* featuring the South County villages of Wakefield and Peace Dale and the University of Rhode Island.

The author lives in South County. She sometimes finds time to post in her blog, *Around ZuZu's Barn, Conversations With Kindred Spirits* which you can find at **www.aroundzuzusbarn.com**

Author's web page: https://claremarypsweeney.carrd.co
Facebook: https://www.facebook.com/cpsweeneyauthor

Books by Claremary P. Sweeney

South County Mystery Series featuring Detective Lieutenant Kara Langley:
Last Train to Kingston - 2017
Last Rose on the Vine - 2018
Last Carol of the Season - 2018
Last Sermon for a Sinner - 2019
Last Castle in the Sand, - 2020

The ZuZu Series – set in the Berkshires of Massachusetts, featuring ZuZu, a charming little tabby:
A Berkshire Tale (10 stories) - 2015
The Pacas Are Coming! ZuZu and the Crias - 2016

Carnivore Conundrum – 2017
A whimsical, illustrated verse tale set at the Roger Williams Park Botanical Center in Cranston, Rhode Island. After a stressful incident with a fly stuck in his digestive juices, Adonis, a tiny pitcher plant, decides he is swearing off meat. His mother and the other plants and creatures in the garden explain the conundrum - he is, after all, a carnivorous plant. But Adonis believes he must follow his heart. And so, a solution must be found to keep this baby alive.

Made in the USA
Monee, IL
16 July 2021

73003451R00105